MUTANT MESSAGE

DOWN UNDER

MUTANT MESSAGE

DOWN UNDER

MARLO MORGAN

Illustrated by Carri Garrison

Element
An Imprint of HarperCollins*Publishers*
77–85 Fulham Palace Road,
Hammersmith, London W6 8JB

The website address is:
www.thorsonselement.com

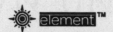

and *Element* are trademarks of
HarperCollins*Publishers* Limited

First published in the USA by HarperCollins*Publishers*, Inc.,
10 East 53rd Street, New York, NY 10022 1994
Thorsons edition 1995

37

A catalogue record for this book
is available from the British Library

ISBN-13 978-1-85538-484-2
ISBN-10 1-85538-484-1

Printed and bound in Great Britain by
Clays Ltd, St Ives plc

This book is dedicated to my mother;
my children, Carri and Steve;
my son-in-law, Greg;
my grandsons, Sean Janning
and Michael Lee;
and most especially to my dad.

CONTENTS

Man did not weave the web of life, he is merely
a strand in it. Whatever he does to the web, he
does to himself.

—American Chief Seattle

The only way to pass any test is to take the test.
It is inevitable.

—Elder Regal Black Swan

Only after the last tree has been cut down. Only
after the last river has been poisoned. Only after
the last fish has been caught. Only then will you
find that money cannot be eaten.

—Cree Indian Prophecy

Born empty handed,
Die empty handed.
I witnessed life at its fullest,
Empty handed.

—Marlo Morgan

ACKNOWLEDGMENTS

This book would not exist if not for two special people—two souls who have taken me under their supportive wings and patiently encouraged me to fly, to soar. My special thanks to Jeannette Grimme and Carri Garrison for sharing in this literary journey at a depth beyond all measuring.

Thank you to author Stephen Mitchell for his gift of sharing and for encouraging me by writing: "If I haven't always translated the words, I have always tried to translate their mind."

Thank you to Og Mandino, Dr. Wayne Dyer, and Dr. Elisabeth Kübler-Ross, all accomplished authors/lecturers and real people.

Thanks to young Marshall Ball for dedicating his life to being a teacher.

I also want to thank Aunt Nola, Dr. Edward J. Stegman, Georgia Lewis, Peg Smith, Dorothea Wolcott, Jenny Decker, Jana Hawkins, Sandford Dean, Nancy Hoflund, Hanley Thomas, Rev. Marilyn Reiger, Rev. Richard Reiger, Walt Bodine, Jack Small, Jeff Small and Wayne Baker at Arrow Printing, Stephanie Gunning and Susan Moldow at Harper-Collins, Robyn Bem, Candice Fuhrman, and most especially MM Co. President Steve Morgan.

FROM THE AUTHOR TO
THE READER

This was written after the fact and inspired by actual experience. As you will see, there wasn't a notebook handy. It is sold as a novel to protect the small tribe of Aborigines from legal involvment. I have deleted details to honor friends who do not wish to be identified and to secure the secret location of our sacred site.

I have saved you a trip to the public library by including important historical information. I can also save you a trip to Australia. The modern-day Aboriginal condition can be seen in any European city, black people living in separate districts of town, well over half on the dole. The employed ones work in menial jobs; their culture appears lost, like the Native American, forced onto designated soil and forbidden for generations to practice all sacred ways.

What I can't save you from is the *Mutant message!*

America, Africa, Australia and Europe all seem to be trying to improve race relations. But somewhere in the dry heat of the Outback there remains a slow, steady, ancient heartbeat, a unique group of people not concerned with racism, but concerned only with other people and the environment. To understand that pulse is to better understand being human or human beingness.

This manuscript was a peaceful self-published work that became controversial. From this reading you could come to several possible conclusions. It might appear to the reader that the man I refer to as my interpreter may not have complied in past years with government rules and regulations: census, taxes, required voting, land use, mining permits, reporting births and deaths, and so on. He may also have aided other tribal citizens in noncompliance. I have been asked to bring this man to the public and to take a group into the desert along the route we walked. I refused! So, one may conclude either that I am guilty of aiding these people in not conforming with the law, or that because I have not produced the actual tribal members, I am lying and the people do not exist.

My answer is this: I do not speak for the Australian Aborigines. I speak only for one small Outback nation referred to as the Wild People or the Ancient Ones. I visited them again, returning to the United States just prior to January 1994. I again received their blessing and approval for how I was handling this assignment.

To you, the reader, I wish to say this: It appears that some people are only ready to be entertained. So if you are one of these people, please read, enjoy, and walk away as you would from any good performance. For you, it is pure fiction, and you will not be disappointed; you will get your money's worth.

If you are, on the other hand, someone who hears the message, it will come through to you loud and strong. You will feel it in your gut, heart, head, and the marrow of your bones. You see, it could easily have been you selected for this walkabout, and believe me many times I wished it had.

We all have our own Outback experiences to grow through; mine just happened to be literally in the Outback. But I did what you would have done, in or out of any shoes.

As your fingers turn these pages, may the people touch your heart. My words are in English but their truth is voiceless.

My suggestion is that you taste the message, savor what is right for you, and spit out the rest; after all, that is the law of the universe.

In the tradition of the desert people, I have also taken another new name to reflect a new talent.

Sincerely,
Traveling Tongue

This book is a work of fiction inspired by my experience in Australia. It could have taken place in Africa or South America or anywhere where the true meaning of civilization is still alive. It is for the reader to receive his or her own message from my story.

—M.M.

1

~~~~~~~~~~~~~~~~~~~~~~~

HONORED GUEST

IT SEEMS there should have been some warning, but I felt none. Events were already in motion. The group of predators sat, miles away, awaiting their prey. The luggage I had unpacked one hour before would tomorrow be tagged "unclaimed" and stay in storage, month after month. I was to become merely one more American to disappear in a foreign country.

It was a sweltering October morning. I stood looking down the drive of the Australian five-star hotel for an unknown courier. Contrary to receiving a warning, my heart was literally singing. I felt so good, so excited, so successful and prepared. Inwardly I sensed, "Today is my day."

A topless jeep pulled into the circular entrance. I remember hearing the tires hiss on the steaming pavement. A fine spray of water leaped over the bordering foliage of brilliant red bottlebrush to touch the rusty metal.

The jeep stopped, and the driver, a thirty-year-old Aborigine, looked my way. "Come on," his black hand beckoned. He was looking for a blond American. I was expecting to be escorted to an Aboriginal tribal meeting. Under the censoring blue eyes and disapproving manner of the uniformed Aussie doorman, we mentally agreed to the match.

Even before I made the awkward struggle of high heels into the all-terrain vehicle, it was obvious I was overdressed. The young driver to my right wore shorts, a dingy white T-shirt, and sockless tennis shoes. I had assumed when they arranged transportation for the meeting, it would be a normal automobile, perhaps a Holden, the pride of Australia's car manufacturers. I never dreamed he would arrive in something wide open. Well, I would rather be overdressed than underdressed to attend a meeting—my award banquet.

I introduced myself. He merely nodded and acted as if he were already certain of who I was. The doorman frowned at us as we propelled past him. We drove through the streets of the coastal city, past rows of veranda-fronted homes, milk-bar snack shops, and grassless cement parks. I clutched the door handle as we circled a roundabout where six directions merged. When we exited, our new heading put the sun at my back. Already the newly acquired, peach-colored business suit and matching silk blouse were becoming uncomfortably warm. I guessed the building was across town, but I was wrong. We entered the main highway running parallel to the sea. This meeting was apparently out of town, further from the hotel than I anticipated. I removed my jacket, thinking how foolish it was not to have asked more questions. At least

I had a brush in my purse, and my shoulder-length bleached hair was pinned up in a fashionable braid.

My curiosity had not subsided from the moment I received the initial phone call, although when it came I couldn't say I was truly surprised. After all, I had received other civic recognitions, and this project had been a major success. Working with urban-dwelling, half-caste Aboriginal adults who had openly displayed suicidal attitudes, and accomplishing for them a sense of purpose and financial success, was bound to be noticed sooner or later. I was surprised; the tribe issuing the summons lived two thousand miles away, on the opposite coast of the continent, but I knew very little about any of the Aboriginal nations except the idle comments I heard occasionally. I didn't know if they were a close-knit race or if, like Native Americans, vast differences, including different languages, were common.

What I really wondered about was what I would receive: another wooden engraved plaque, to be sent back for storage in Kansas City, or perhaps simply a bouquet of flowers? No, not flowers, not in one-hundred-degree weather. That would be too cumbersome to take on the return flight. The driver had arrived promptly, as agreed, at twelve o'clock noon. So I knew, of course, I was in for a luncheon meeting. I wondered what in the world a native council would serve for our meal? I hoped it would not be a catered traditional Australian affair. Perhaps they would have a potluck buffet, and I could sample Aboriginal dishes for the first time. I was hoping to see a table laden with colorful casseroles.

This was going to be a wonderfully unique experience, and I was looking forward to a memorable day. The purse I carried, purchased for today, held a 35-mm camera and a small tape recorder. They hadn't said anything about microphones or spotlights or my giving a speech, but I was prepared anyway. One of my greatest assets was thinking ahead. After all, I was now fifty years old, had suffered enough embarrassment and disappointments in my life to have adopted plans for alternative courses. My friends remarked how self-sufficient I was. "Always has Plan B up her sleeve," I could hear them saying.

A highway road train (the Australian term for a truck pulling numerous full-sized trailers in convoy style) passed us heading in the opposite direction. They came bolting out of fuzzy heat waves, straight down the center of the pavement. I was shaken back from my memories when the driver jerked the steering wheel and we left the highway, heading down a rugged dirt road, followed for miles by a fog of red dust. Somewhere, the two well-worn ruts disappeared, and I became aware there was no longer a road in front of us. We were zigzagging around bushes and jumping over the serrated, sandy desert. I tried to make conversation several times, but the noise of the open vehicle, the brush from the underside of the chassis, and the movement of my body up and down, made it impossible. It was necessary to hold my jaws tightly together to keep from biting my tongue. Obviously the driver had no interest in opening the portals of speech.

My head bounced as if my body were a child's cloth doll. I was getting hotter and hotter. My pantyhose felt like they were melted on my feet, but I was afraid to remove a shoe for fear it would bounce out into the expanse of copper-colored flatness surrounding us as far as the eye could see. I had no faith the mute driver would stop. Every time my sunglasses became filmed over I wiped them off with the hem of my slip. The movement of my arms let open the floodgate to a river of perspiration. I could feel my makeup dissolve and pictured the rosy tinge once painted on my cheeks now streaking as red trails down my neck. They would have to allow me twenty minutes to get myself back in order before the presentation. I would insist on it!

I studied my watch; two hours had passed since entering the desert. I was hotter and more uncomfortable than I could remember feeling in years. The driver remained silent except for an occasional hum. It suddenly dawned on me: He had not introduced himself. Maybe I wasn't in the correct vehicle! But that was silly. I couldn't get out, and he certainly seemed confident about me as a passenger.

Four hours later, we pulled up to a corrugated tin structure. A small, smoldering fire burned outside, and two Aboriginal women stood up as we approached. They were both middle-aged, short, scantily clad, wearing warm smiles of welcome. One wore a headband that made her thick, curly black hair escape at strange angles. They both appeared slim and athletic, with round, full faces holding bright brown eyes. As I descended from the jeep, my chauffeur said, "By the way, I am the only one who speaks English. I will be your interpreter, your friend."

"Great!" I thought to myself. "I've spent seven hundred dollars on airfare, hotel room, and new clothes for this introduction to native Australians, and now I find out they can't even speak English, let alone recognize current fashions."

Well, I was here, so I might as well try to blend in, although in my heart I knew I could not.

The women spoke in blunt foreign sounds that did not seem like sentences, only single words. My interpreter turned to me and explained that permission to attend the meeting required I first be cleansed. I did not understand what he meant. It was true I was covered with several layers of dust and hot from the ride, but that did not seem to be his meaning. He handed me a piece of cloth, which I opened to discover had the appearance of a wraparound rag. I was told I needed to remove my clothing and put it on. "What?" I asked, unbelieving. "Are you serious?" He sternly repeated the instructions. I looked around for a place to change; there was none. What could I do? I had come too far and endured too much discomfort at this point to decline. The young man walked away. "Oh, what the heck. It will be cooler than these clothes," I thought. So, as discreetly as possible, I removed my soiled new clothing, folded it neatly into a pile, and donned the native attire. I stacked my things on the nearby boulder, which only moments before had served as a stool for the waiting women. I felt silly in the colorless rag and regretted investing in the new "making a good impression" clothing. The young man reappeared. He, too, had changed clothing. He stood before me almost naked, having only a cloth wrapped around in swimming trunk fashion and barefoot, as were the women at the fire. He issued further instructions to remove everything: shoes, hose, undergarments, and all my jewelry, even the bobby pins holding my hair. My curiosity was slowly fading, and apprehension was taking over, but I did as told.

I remember stuffing my jewelry into the toe of my

shoe. I also did something that seems to come naturally to females, although I am sure we are not taught to do it; I placed my underwear in the middle of the stack of clothing.

A blanket of thick gray smoke rose from the smoldering coals as fresh green brush was added. The headbanded woman took what appeared to be the wing from a large black hawk and opened it to form a fan. She flapped it in front of me from face to feet. The smoke swirled, stifling my breath. Next she motioned with an index finger in a circular pattern, which I understood to mean "turn around." The smoke ritual was repeated behind me. Then I was instructed to step across the fire, through the smoke.

Finally I was told I had been cleansed and received permission to enter the metal shed. As the bronze male escort walked with me around to the entrance, I saw the same woman pick up my entire stack of belongings. She held it up above the flames. She looked at me, smiled, and as our eyes acknowledged one another, she released the treasures in her hands. Everything I owned went into the fire!

For a moment my heart was numb; I took a very deep sigh. I don't know why I didn't shout a protest and immediately run to retrieve everything. But I didn't. The woman's facial expression indicated her action was not malicious; it was done in the manner one might offer a stranger some unique sign of hospitality. "She is just ignorant," I thought. "Doesn't understand about credit cards and important papers." I was grateful I had left my airline ticket at the hotel. I knew I had other clothes there too, and somehow I would deal with walking through the lobby dressed in this garb when the time came. I remember thinking to myself, "Hey, Marlo, you are a flexible person. This isn't worth getting an ulcer over." But I did make a mental note to dig one of the rings from the ashes later. Hopefully, the fire would die down and cool off before our return jeep ride back into the city.

But that was not to be.

Only in retrospect would I understand the symbology being played out as I removed my valuable and what I considered very necessary jewelry. I was yet to learn that time for these people had absolutely nothing to do with the clock hours on the gold-and-diamond watch now donated to the earth forever.

Much later I would understand that the releasing of attachment to objects and certain beliefs was already indelibly written as a very necessary step in my human progress toward *being*.

2

<hr />

STUFFING THE BALLOT BOX

WE ENTERED the open side of the three-sided, roofed shed. There was no actual door or need for windows. It was simply constructed for the purpose of shade, or perhaps as a haven for sheep. Inside, the heat was intensified by another fire encircled in stone. There were no signs of its providing for human needs: no chairs, no flooring, no fan; it was without electricity. The entire place was rippling tin held together precariously by worn and rotting lumber.

My eyes adjusted quickly from the glare I had been experiencing the last four hours to the darker hue of the shade and smoke. A group of adult Aboriginal people were standing or sitting on the sand. The males wore colorful, ornate headbands and had feathers attached both to their upper arms and around their ankles. They wore the same type of wrap as the driver. He was unpainted, but the others had designs painted on their faces and along their arms and legs. They had used white to make dots, stripes, and elaborate patterns. Drawings of lizards adorned their arms while snakes, kangaroos, and birds appeared upon legs and backs.

The women were less festive. They appeared to be about my height—five-six. Most were elderly but had creamy milk-chocolate skin, appearing soft and healthy. I saw no one with long hair; most of it was curly and closely cropped to their scalp. Those who appeared to have much length to their hair wore a narrow band that crisscrossed around their head and held it down firmly. One very old, white-haired lady near the entrance had a garland of flowers hand-painted around her neck and ankles. It had the artist's touch, with detailed leaves and stamen portrayed in the center of each blossom. All were wearing either two pieces of cloth or a wraparound garment like the one they had given me. I saw no babies or young children, only one teenage boy.

My eyes were drawn to the most elaborately attired person in the room—a man, his black hair flecked with gray. His trim beard accentuated the strength and dignity of his face. On his head was a stunning full headdress made of bright parrot feathers. He, too, wore feathers on his arms and ankles. There were several objects strapped around his waist, and he wore a circular, intricately crafted chest plate made from stone and seeds. Several of the women had similar, smaller versions worn as necklaces.

He smiled and held out both hands to me. As I looked into his black velvet eyes, I had a feeling of complete peace and security. I think he had the most gentle face I have ever witnessed.

My emotions, however, were stretched in straining

opposition. The painted faces, and the men standing around the back clutching razor-sharp spears, supported my growing sense of fear. Yet, everyone wore a pleasant expression, and the atmosphere seemed to release an aroma of nourishing comfort and friendship. I settled emotionally midstream, by judging my own stupidity. This did not resemble even a token of what I had expected. Never in a dream could I have invented such a threatening atmosphere holding so many seemingly gentle people. If only my camera weren't engulfed in flames outside this shack; what great photos I could paste in an album or show as slides to some future captive audience of relatives or friends. My thoughts returned to the fire. What else was burning up? I shuddered at the thought: my international driver's permit, orange Australian paper money, the one-hundred-dollar bill I had carried for years in a secret compartment of my wallet that dated back to my youthful, telephone-company employment days, a favorite tube of creamy lipstick unobtainable in this country, my diamond watch, and the ring Aunt Nola had given me for my eighteenth birthday, were all fueling the fire.

My anxiety was interrupted as I was introduced to the tribe by the interpreter, whose name was Ooota. He pronounced it with "Ooo" drawn out almost like "Oooooo" and then ended abruptly "ta."

The brotherly man with the incredible eyes was referred to by the Aborigines as Tribal Elder. He was not the oldest male of the group but more like our definition of a chief.

One woman began clicking sticks together and was soon joined by another and another. The spear bearers

began thumping the tall shafts in the sand and still others
were clapping hands. The whole group began to sing and
chant. By hand gesture I was invited to sit down on the
sandy floor. The group was putting on a *corroboree*, or
festival. At the conclusion of one song, another would
begin. I had not noticed before that some of the people
had ankle bracelets made of large pods, but now they
became focal points as the encased dried seeds became
pulsing rattles. At one point there was a single female
dancer, then a group. Sometimes the men danced alone
and at other times women joined them. They were sharing
their history with me.

Finally the tempo of the music slowed, the movements
wound down to a much slower pace. Then all the movement ceased. Only a very steady beat, one that seemed
synchronized to the pulse of my heart, remained. All the
people were silent and still. They looked toward their
leader. He stood up and walked to me. Smiling, he stood
before me. There was an indescribable sense of communion. I had the intuitive feeling we were old friends, but of
course that was not true. I guessed his presence just made
me feel comfortable and accepted.

The Elder took off a long leather tube of platypus
hide strapped to his waist and shook it at the sky. He
opened the end and threw the contents out onto the
ground. There were rocks, bones, teeth, feathers, and
round leather discs lying around me. Several members of
the tribe helped mark where each item landed. They were
as adept at using a toe as a finger on the earthen floor to
make the marks. Then they put the items back into the
case. The Elder said something and handed it to me. I was
reminded of Las Vegas, so I too held the tube up in the air

and shook it. I repeated the game by opening the end and throwing the contents, feeling absolutely no control over where each landed. Two men on hands and knees used the foot of another to measure where my items had fallen in comparison to the Elder's. A few comments were passed among several people, but Ooota did not offer to tell me what was being said.

We did several tests that afternoon. One very impressive one involved a piece of fruit. It was something with a thick skin like a banana but shaped like a pear. I was given the light green fruit and told to hold it, to bless it. What did that mean? I had no idea, so mentally I simply said, "Please, dear Lord, bless this food," and handed it back to the Elder. He took a knife, cut the top, and started to peel it. Instead of the peeling falling down like a banana skin does, this outer coat curled around. When it did, all faces pivoted in my direction. I felt uncomfortable with dark eyes staring at me. In unison, as if they had practiced, all said, "Ah." It happened each time the Elder pulled down the peel. I did not know if the "Ah" was a good "Ah" or a bad "Ah," but I seemed to sense that the peel did not normally curl when cut, and whatever the tests were indicating, I was scoring a passing mark.

A young woman came to me holding a plate full of rocks. It was probably a piece of cardboard rather than a plate, but it was piled so high with stones I could not see the container. Ooota looked at me very seriously and said, "Choose a rock. Choose it wisely. It has the power to save your life."

Goose bumps appeared instantly although my limbs were hot and sweaty. My gut reacted with a question in its own language. The knotted stomach muscles signaled, "What does that mean? Power to save my life!"

I looked at the rocks. They all looked alike. There was nothing outstanding about any of them. They were simply gray-red pebbles about the size of a nickel or quarter. I wished something would glow or look special. No luck. So I faked it: I looked intently as if I were studying them seriously, and then I selected one from the top and held it up triumphantly. The faces surrounding me beamed in approval, and in mental silence I rejoiced, "I got the right rock!"

But what should I do with it? I couldn't drop it and hurt their feelings. After all, this stone meant nothing to me but seemed important to them. I had no pocket to put it in, so I stuck it down the front of my current covering in the chest cleavage, which was the only place I could think to put it. I promptly forgot the contents secured in nature's pocket.

Next they put out the fire, dismantled the instruments, gathered up their few possessions, and started walking out into the desert. Their brown, nearly naked torsos sparkled in the bright sun as they filed into journey position. It seemed the meeting was over: no lunch, no award! Ooota was the last to leave, but he too was walking away. After several yards he turned and said, "Come. We are leaving now."

"Where are we going?" I inquired.

"On a walkabout."

"Where are you walking to?"

"Across Australia."

"Great! How long will this take?"

"Approximately three full changes of the moon."

"Are you saying, walk for three months?"

"Yes, three months, more or less."

I sighed deeply. Then I announced to Ooota as he stood in the distance: "Well, that sounds like a lot of fun, but you see, I can't go. Today is just not a good day for me to leave. I have responsibilities, obligations, rent, utility bills. I have made no preparations. I would need time to make arrangements before I could take off on a hike or camping trip. Perhaps you don't understand: I am not an Australian citizen; I am American. We can't just go to a foreign country and disappear. Your immigration officials would be upset, and my government would send out helicopters looking for me. Maybe some other time, when I have plenty of advance warning, I could join you, but not today. I just can't go with you today. No, today is just not a good day."

Ooota smiled. "All is in order. Everyone will know who needs to know. My people heard your cry for help. If anyone in this tribe had voted against you, they would not walk this journey. You have been tested and accepted. The extreme honor I cannot explain. You must live the experience. It is the most important thing you will do in this lifetime. It is what you were born to do. Divine Oneness is at work; it is your message. I can tell you no more.

"Come. Follow." He turned and walked away.

I stood there staring out across the Australian desert. It was vast, desolate, and yet beautiful, and like the Energizer battery, it seemed to go on and on and on. The jeep was there, ignition key in it. But which way had we come? There had been no road for hours, only endless twisting and turning. I had no shoes, no water, no food.

The temperature this time of year in the desert ranged between 100 and 130 degrees. I was glad they had voted to accept me, but what about my vote? It seemed to me the decision was not in my hands.

I did not want to go. They were asking me to put my life in their hands. These were people I had just met, and with whom I couldn't even talk. What if I lost my employment position? It is bad enough; already my future held no security from any company retirement check! It was insane! Of course I couldn't go!

I thought, "I'll bet this is a two-part deal. First they play games here in this shack, then they go out into the desert and play some more. They aren't going very far; they have no food. The worst thing that could happen to me would be expecting me to spend the night out there. But no," I thought, "they can take one look at me and see I am not a camper; I am a city bubble-bath type! But," I went on, "I can if I have to! I will simply be assertive since I have already paid for one night at the hotel. I will tell them they must return me before checkout time tomorrow. I'm not going to pay for an extra day just to satisfy these silly uneducated folks."

I watched the group walking further and further away and appearing smaller and smaller. I didn't have time for my Libra method of weighing advantages and disadvantages. The longer I stood there thinking about what to do, the further out of sight they were becoming. The exact words I said are embedded in my brain as clearly as a beautifully polished wooden inlay might appear. "Okay, God. I know you have a really funny sense of humor, but I don't understand this one at all!"

With feelings that rapidly ping-ponged between fear,

amazement, disbelief, and sheer numbness, I began to follow the tribe of Aborigines who call themselves Real People.

I wasn't bound and gagged, but I felt like a captive. To me, it appeared, I was the victim of a forced march into the unknown.

3

~~~~~~~~~~~~~~~

NATURAL FOOTWEAR

I HAD walked only a short distance when I felt stabbing pain in my feet and looked down to see barbs protruding from my skin. I pulled out the piercing thorns only to find each time I took a step, more reentered. I tried to hop on one foot in a forward pace and extract the painful sticker from the other at the same time. It must have appeared comical to the members of the group who turned to look back. Their smiles were now full grins. Ooota had stopped to wait for me, and his facial expression appeared more sympathetic as he said, "Forget the pain. Remove the thorns when we camp. Learn to endure. Focus your attention elsewhere. We will help your feet later. You can do nothing now."

It was his words "Focus your attention elsewhere" that were significant to me. I have worked with hundreds of people in pain, especially in the last fifteen years as a doctor specializing in acupuncture. Often in terminal situations the person must decide between some drug that renders them unconscious or the use of acupuncture. In my house-call educational program I have used those exact words. I have expected my patients to be able to do it, and now someone was expecting it of me. It was easier said than done, but I managed.

After a while, we stopped to rest for a few moments, and I found most of the tips had broken off. The cuts were bleeding, and splinters were embedded under my skin. We were walking on spinifex. It is what botanists refer to as beach grass, binding to the sand and surviving where there is little water by developing rolled, steak-knife sharp blades. The word *grass* is very deceiving. This stuff doesn't resemble any grass to which I could relate. Not only were the blades cutting, the barbs on them are like cactus tips. When they entered my skin, they left a stinging, swollen red irritation. Fortunately I am a semi-ourdoor person, enjoying a moderate suntan and often walking barefoot, but my soles were not nearly prepared for the abuse ahead. Pain continued, and blood in all shades from bright red to dark brown appeared at the surface of my feet, even though I was trying to put my attention elsewhere. Looking down, I could no longer distinguish the ragged polish on my toenails from the red color of my blood. Finally my feet became numb.

We walked in complete silence. It seemed very strange, no one talking at all. The sand was warm, not beastly hot. The sun was hot, but not unbearable. Periodically the world seemed to take pity on me and provide a brief breeze of cooler air. As I looked ahead of the group, there seemed to be no clearly defined line between earth and sky. The same scene was repeated in all directions, like a watercolor painting, with the sky melting into the sand. My scientific mind wanted to appease the blankness with a compass. A cloud formation thousands of feet overhead seemed to make one lone tree on the horizon appear as a dotted "i." I heard only the crunching sound of feet on the earth as though strips of Velcro were repeatedly separated and reunited. The monotony was occasionally broken by some desert creature moving in nearby brush. A large brown falcon appeared out of nowhere and circled, swooping over my head. Somehow I felt he was checking my personal progress. He did not swoop at any of the others. But I looked so different from everyone else, I could understand why, perhaps, he needed closer inspection.

Without warning, the whole column of people stopped walking forward and turned off on an angle. It surprised me; I heard no words directing us to change course. Everyone seemed to sense it except me. I thought perhaps they had this trail down pat, but it was obvious we were not following a path in the sand and spinifex. We were wandering in the desert.

My head was a whirl of thoughts. In the silence it was easy for me to observe my thoughts fleeing from subject to subject.

Was this really happening? Maybe it is a dream. They said walk across Australia. That isn't possible! Walk for months! That isn't reasonable either. They heard my cry for help. What did that mean? This is something I was born to do! What a joke. It wasn't my life's ambition to suffer, exploring the Outback. I also worried about the concern my disappearance would cause my children, especially my daughter. We were very close. I thought about

my landlady, who was a grand elderly matron. If I didn't
pay my rent on time, she would help me straighten it out
with the property owners. Only last week I had leased a
television and VCR. Well, repossession would be a unique
experience!

At that point, I couldn't believe we would be gone for
more than a day at the most. After all, there was nothing
to eat or drink in sight.

I laughed aloud. A private joke. How many times I
had said I wanted to win an exotic all-expenses-paid trip!
Here it was. All provisions were supplied. I didn't even
have to pack a toothbrush or a change of clothes. It was
not what I had in mind, but it certainly was what I had
verbalized time and time again.

As the day wore on, there were so many cuts on the
bottom and sides of my feet that the slits, hardened
blood, and swollen circles combined into ugly, numb,
discolored extremities. My legs were stiff, shoulders
burned and aching, face and arms red and raw. We
walked about three hours that day. The limitations of
my endurance were expanded over and over. At times I
felt that if I did not sit down soon I would collapse.
Then something would happen to attract my attention.
The falcon would appear, making its strange eerie
screech over my head, or someone would walk next to
me and offer me a drink of water from an unfamiliar-
looking nonpottery vessel tied to a rope around the
neck or waist. Miraculously the distraction always provided wings, carrying new strength, a second wind.
Finally, it was time to stop for the night.

Everyone was immediately busy. A fire was lit, using
not matches but a method I recalled seeing in the Girl

Scout Wilderness Manual. I had never tried twirling a stick in a slotted groove to spark a fire. Our scout leaders couldn't get it to work. They could barely get it hot enough to ignite the tiny flame, and blowing on it only worked to cool, not spread, the heat. These people, however, were experts. Some gathered firewood and others gathered plants. Two men had been jointly sharing a load all afternoon. They had a colorless cloth draped over two long spears and made into a pouch. It held contents that bulged like giant marbles as we walked. Now they set it down and removed several items.

A very old woman approached me. She looked as old as my grandmother—in her nineties. Her hair was snowy white. Soft, folded wrinkles filled her face. Her body appeared to be lean, strong, and smoothly supple, but her feet were so dry and hard they had developed into almost a sort of animal hoof. She was the one I had seen earlier with the elaborately painted necklace and ankle ornament. Now she took off a little snakeskin pouch tied at her waist and poured something that looked like discolored vasoline into the palm of her hand. I learned it was a leaf oil mixture. She pointed to my feet and I nodded an agreement for help. She sat in front of me, took my feet into her lap, rubbed the ointment into my swollen sores, and sang a song. It was a soothing melody, almost like a mother's lullaby for her babe. I asked Ooota what her words meant.

"She is apologizing to your feet. She is telling them how much you appreciate them. She is telling how much everyone in this group appreciates your feet, and she is asking your feet to get well and strong. She makes special sounds for healing wounds and cuts. She also tones sounds that draw out the swelling fluids. She asks that your feet become very strong and tough."

It wasn't my imagination. The burning, stinging, raw sores really did began to ease, and I felt gradual relief.

As I sat with my feet in this grandmotherly lap, I began mentally to challenge the reality of today's experience. How did this happen? Where had it all started?

4

~~~~~~~~~~~~~~~~~~~

READY, SET, GO

IT STARTED in Kansas City. The memory of the exact morning is etched forever in my mind. The sun had decided to honor us with its presence after being undercover for several days. I had gone to the office early to plan for patients with special needs. The receptionist wouldn't be in for two hours, and I always treasured this quiet time of preparation.

As my key clicked in the outside door, I heard the phone ringing. Was there some emergency? Who would call this much ahead of office hours? I rushed to my inner office, grabbing the phone with one hand and flipping the light switch with the other.

A man's excited voice greeted me. He was an Australian whom I had met at a physician's conference in California. He was calling now from Australia.

"Ga-dye. How would you like to work in Australia for a few years?"

Speechless, I almost dropped the phone.

"Are you still there?" questioned the caller.

"Y-y-yes," I managed to stammer. "Tell me what you have in mind."

"I was so impressed with your unique patient-education program for preventive health that I told my mates here about you. They asked me to call. We want you to try and obtain a five-year visa and come here. You could write training material and teach in our socialized health-care system. It would be wonderful if we could get it implemented, and anyway, it would give you an opportunity to live in a foreign country for a few years."

The suggestion of leaving my contemporary lake-property home, a securely established health practice, and patients who had become close friends over the years was a thrust into my comfort zone as foreign as the nail must feel entering the plank. It was true I was very curious about socialized medicine, in which you eliminate profit from the health-care system, where disciplines work together without the Grand Canyon between medicine and natural practitioners. Would I find peers truly dedicated to health and healing, to doing whatever works, or would I find myself involved in merely a new form of negative manipulation, like the politics of treating disease has become in the United States?

What excited me most was simply Australia. As far back into childhood as I could remember I had been drawn to read every book I could find about the land Down Under. Unfortunately there were few. At the zoo I was always seeking out the kangaroo, and searching for the rare chance I might see a koala. On some mysteriously hidden level, it was a quest I had always dreamed to answer. I felt I was a confident, educated female, self-supporting, and for as long as I could remember there had been a yearning in my soul, a tug at my heart, to visit the land on the bottom of the globe.

"Think about it," urged the Australian voice. "I'll ring you back in a fortnight."

Talk about timing. Only two weeks before, my daughter and her fiancé had set a wedding date. That meant that for the first time in my adult life I was free to live any place on earth I chose and to do anything I truly desired. Both my son and daughter would be fully supportive as usual. They had, after the divorce, become more like two close friends than my children. Now they were both young adults on their own, and I was experiencing a wish becoming reality.

Six weeks later, the wedding celebrated and my health practice in new hands, my daughter and a dear friend stood with me at the airport. It was a strange feeling. For the first time in years I had no car, no home, no keys; even my luggage had combination locks. I had disposed of all my worldly possessions except for a few things in storage. The family heirlooms were safely placed in the care of my sister, Patci. My friend Jana handed me a book, and we hugged. My daughter, Carri, took one last photo, and I walked down the red-carpet ramp toward an experience on the continent Down Under. I did not anticipate the magnitude of the lessons in store. My mother used to tell me, "Choose wisely, for what you ask may very well be what you receive." Although she had passed away years before, that very day marked the true beginning of my understanding of her oft-repeated phrase.

The flight to Australia from the Midwest is an

extremely long one. Fortunately for travelers, even the big jets require fuel stops occasionally, so we were allowed to breathe fresh air as we took on supplies in Hawaii and again in Fiji. The Qantas jet was spacious. The movies were current top-rated American cinema. Still, the trip felt extended.

Australia is seventeen hours ahead of the United States. It is literally flying into tomorrow. During the trip, I reminded myself that we knew for certain that tomorrow the world would still be intact and functioning! It was already tomorrow on the land mass ahead. No wonder sailors of old celebrated robustly when they crossed the equator and the imaginary line on the sea where time begins. The concept today is still a mind-expanding one.

When we reached the Australian soil, the entire plane and all passengers were sprayed for possible contaminants to this isolated continent. The travel agent had not prepared me for this. As the plane landed, we were told to remain seated. Two ground-crew employees walked from the cockpit to the tail of the craft using aerosol cans above our heads. I understood the Australian reasoning, but somehow the comparison of my body to a destructive insect was demoralizing.

Quite a welcome!

Outside the airport, the scene looked like home. In fact, I would have thought I was still in the United States except the traffic was zipping along in a direction opposite ours. The taxi driver was seated behind the steering column on the right. He suggested a foreign exchange booth where I purchased dollar bills too large to fit into my American wallet but much more colorful and decorative than our greenbacks, and I discovered wonderful two- and twenty-cent coins.

Over the next few days, I found getting accustomed to Australia no problem at all. All the major cities are on the coasts. Everyone is interested in the beach and water sports. The country has almost the same square miles as the United States and is similarly shaped, but the interior is isolated wasteland. I was familiar with our Painted Desert and Death Valley. However, the Aussies sometimes find it difficult to picture the heart of our country growing wheat and rows and rows of tall yellow corn. Their interior is so unsupportive to human life that the Royal Flying Doctor Service remains on constant call. The pilots are even sent on rescue missions with petrol or automobile parts for stranded motorists. People are flown in airplanes to receive medical attention. There are no hospitals for hundreds of miles. Even the school system has education by radio available for the youngsters in the remote regions.

I found the cities very modern, with Hilton, Holiday Inn, and Ramada hotels, shopping malls, designer clothing, and rapid transit. The food was different. In my opinion, they are still learning to make some basic imitations of American favorites but I found wonderful shepherd's pie like I had in England. They rarely served water with meals and never with ice cubes.

I love the people and their different expressions:

Fair dinkum for okay or the real thing
chook, chicken
chips, french fries.
sheila, young girl

lolly, candy; *sweets,* dessert
bush, rural area
tinny, a can of beer
joey, infant kangaroo
biscuit, cookie
swag, a bedroll or backpack.
walkabout, leaving for unknown period
having a crook day, having a bad day
tucker, food
footpath, sidewalk
billibong, a watering hole
boot, trunk of a car; *bonnet,* the hood
serviette, a table napkin

It seemed odd in the stores that they said thank you before they said please. "That will be one dollar, thank you," the clerk remarks.

Beer is a great national treasure. Personally, I have never cared for beer, so I didn't try the variety of which they are so proud. Each of the Australian states has a brewery, and people are very sensitive in their loyalty, for example, to Foster's Lager or Four X.

The Australians have specific words they use for different nationalities. They often refer to Americans as Yanks, to a New Zealand citizen as a Kiwi, and to the British as Bloody Poms. One authority told me that "pom" referred to the red plumage worn by the European military, but someone else said it originated from the initials POM appearing on the clothing of the nineteenth-century convict arrivals; POM meant Prisoner of His Majesty.

Of all the things I love about Australians, I love the

singsong tempo of their speech most. Of course, they told me I was the one with an accent. I found the Australians to be very friendly, making strangers feel at home and immediately welcome.

The first few days I tried out several hotels. Each time I checked in, they handed me a small metal pitcher of milk. I observed each guest receiving one. In the room I found an electric teapot, tea bags, and sugar. It seems the Aussies love tea with milk and sugar. It did not take me long to discover that a cup of American-tasting coffee was not obtainable.

The first time I tried a motel, the elderly owner asked if I wanted to order breakfast and showed me a handwritten menu. I did, so he then asked what time I wanted it prepared. He advised me it would be brought to my room. The next morning as I was taking a bath, I heard footsteps approach my door but not enter. I waited for a knock but none came. I did hear a strange noise like a slamming door. As I was drying myself, I began to smell food. I looked all around; there wasn't any. But I definitely smelled food. It must be coming from next door, I reasoned.

I spent about an hour preparing for the day and repacking my suitcase. As I was loading my suitcase into the rental car, a young man came up the sidewalk.

"Ga-dye, was your meal all right?" he asked.

I smiled. "There must have been some mixup. I didn't receive any breakfast."

"Oh, yes, it is right here. I delivered it myself," he said, as he walked over to a knob on the outer wall of the motel room and lifted it. Inside a little compartment was a beautifully garnished platter of rubbery cold scrambled eggs. He then walked inside the room and opened a cupboard door to display the dismal sight again. We both laughed. I could smell it; I just couldn't find it. It was the beginning of many surprises Australia held for me.

The Aussies were kind. I found them gracious when helping me locate a house to rent. It was in a well-kept suburban area. All of the homes in the neighborhood were built about the same time—all one-story, white, with front and side porches. None had locks on the doors originally. The bathroom facilities were divided, with the toilet in a little closet and the bathtub and wash basin in a separate room. I also had no built-in closet space but was provided with old-fashioned freestanding wardrobes. None of my U.S. appliances would work. The electricity is different, and the plugs are shaped differently. I had to purchase a new hair dryer and curling iron.

The backyard was filled with exotic flowers and trees. Because of the warm weather, they bloom all year. At night, cane toads came to enjoy the foliage perfume, and they seemed to increase in number over the months—they are a national nuisance, their population completely out of control, and so must be stabbed and controlled at a neighborhood level. My yard was apparently a safe haven.

The Australians introduced me to lawn bowling, an outdoor sport where all players wear white. I had passed stores selling nothing but white shirts, white pants and skirts, white shoes and socks, even white hats. It was nice at last to find an answer for such strange and limited merchandise. They also took me to an Australian Rules football game. It was really rough. All the football players I had ever seen wore heavy padding, helmets, and were fully covered. These fellows wore short pants, short-sleeved shirts, and no pads. On the beach I saw people wearing rubber hats that tied under their chins. I learned this indicated the person was a lifesaver. They also have special shark-patrol lifesavers. Being eaten by a shark is not a common occurrence but is enough of a problem to warrant the special training.

Australia is the world's flattest and driest continent. The mountains adjacent to the coasts cause most rainfall to run toward the sea and leave 90 percent of the land semiarid. You can travel by air two thousand miles from Sydney to Perth and see no towns.

I traveled to all the major cities of the continent because of the health project with which I was involved. In the United States, I had a special microscope that could be used with whole blood, not altered or separated. By viewing a drop of whole blood, it is possible to see many aspects of patients' chemistry graphically in movement. We connected the microscope to a video camera and monitor screen. Sitting next to the physician, patients could see their white cells, red cells, bacteria, or fat in the background. I would take samples, show the patients their blood, and then ask smokers, for instance, to step outside and have a cigarette. After only a few moments, we would draw another sample, and they could see what effects that one cigarette had. The system is used for patient education and is very powerful in motivating them toward becoming responsible for their own welfare. Physicians can use it for many conditions, such as showing patients the level of fat in their blood or a sluggish immune response, and then can talk to the patients about what they can do to help themselves. However, in the United States, our insurance companies won't cover costs for preventive measures, so patients have to pay out of pocket.

We hoped the Australian system would be more receptive. My assignment involved demonstrating the technique, importing and securing equipment, writing instructions, and ultimately doing the training. It was a very worthwhile project, and I was having a wonderful time in the land Down Under.

One Saturday afternoon I went to the science museum. The tour guide was a large, expensively dressed female who was curious about the United States. We chatted and soon became good friends. One day she recommended we meet for lunch and suggested a quaint tearoom in the heart of the city that advertised fortune-tellers. I remember sitting in the shop waiting for the appearance of my friend and thinking I was always on time, so why did I seem to have an aura of magnetism that attracts friends with constantly late personalities? Closing time approached. She wasn't going to show up. I bent to pick up my purse from the floor where I had placed it forty-five minutes earlier.

A young man—tall, thin, dark-complexioned, dressed in white from sandaled feet to turbaned head—walked up to the table.

"I have time to give your reading now," he stated in a quiet voice.

"Oh, I was waiting for a friend. But it doesn't seem she was able to make it today. I'll be back."

"Sometimes that works out for the best," he commented as he pulled out the chair across from me at the small round table for two. He sat down and took my hand in his. Turning it palm up, he began his reading. He didn't look at my hand; his eyes remained fixed looking into mine.

"The reason you have come to this place, not this tearoom but this continent, is destiny. There is someone here you have agreed to meet for your mutual benefit. The agreement was made before either of you were born. In fact, you chose to be born at the same instant, one on the top of the world and the other here, Down Under. The pact was made on the highest level of your eternal self. You agreed not to seek one another until fifty years had passed. It is now time. When you meet, there will be instant recognition on a soul level. That is all I can tell you."

He stood up and walked away through the door I assumed went into the restaurant kitchen. I was speechless. Nothing he said made any sense whatsoever, but he spoke with such authority, somehow I was compelled to take it to heart.

The incident became more complicated when my friend called that evening to apologize and explain why she had not kept our luncheon appointment. She became excited when I told her what had happened, and she vowed the following day to seek the reader and receive information about her own future.

When she phoned the next time, her enthusiasm had changed to doubt. "The tearoom has no male readers," she told me. "They have a different person each day, but all are women. On Tuesday it was Rose, and she doesn't read palms. She reads cards. Are you sure you went to the right place?"

I knew I wasn't crazy. I have always considered fortune-telling as purely entertainment, but one thing was for certain; the young man was not an illusion. Oh well, Aussies think Yanks are flakes anyway. Besides, no one seriously considers it anything except fun, and Australia was full of fun things to do for entertainment.

5

GETTING HIGH

THERE WAS only one thing about the country I did not enjoy. It appeared to me the original people of the land, the dark-skinned natives called Aborigines, were still experiencing discrimination. They were treated much the same way as we Americans treated our native people. The land they were given to live on in the Outback is worthless sand, and the area in the northern territory is rugged cliff and scrub brush. The only reasonable area considered still their land is also designated as national parks, so they live sharing it with the tourists.

I did not see any Aborigines at social functions, nor any walking along the streets with uniformed schoolchildren. I saw none at Sunday church services, though I attended different denominations. I did not see any working as grocery clerks, handling packages at the post office, or selling goods in the department stores. I visited government offices and saw no Aboriginal employees. I couldn't find any working at gas stations or waiting on customers at the chain fast-food shops. There appeared to be few of them. They were visible in the city, performing at the tourist centers. Vacationers observed them on the Australian-owned sheep and cattle paddocks working as helpers, called Jackaroos. I was told when a rancher occasionally finds an indication that a wandering group of Aborigines have killed a sheep, he does not file charges. The natives only take what they truly need to eat, and quite frankly they are credited with supernatural powers of retaliation.

One evening I observed a group of young half-caste Aborigines in their early twenties putting petrol into cans, then inhaling it as they walked downtown. They became visibly intoxicated from the fumes. Petrol is a mixture of hydrocarbons and chemicals. I knew they were potentially destructive to bone marrow, liver, kidneys, adrenal glands, the spinal cord, and the entire central nervous system. But like everyone else on the plaza that night, I didn't do anything. I didn't say anything. I made no attempt to stop their stupid play. Later, I learned that one of those I had witnessed had died of lead toxicity and respiratory failure. I felt the loss as deeply as I would have felt burying a longtime friend. I went to the morgue and viewed the tragic remains. As someone who was spending my life trying to prevent illness, it seemed that the loss of culture and loss of personal purpose must have been contributing factors in the gambling with death. What bothered me most was that I had watched and didn't raise a finger to stop them. I questioned my new Aussie friend, Geoff. He was the owner of a large automobile dealership, my age, unmarried, and very attractive—the Robert Redford of

Australia. We had been on several dates, so at one can-
dlelit dinner following the symphony, I asked him if the
citizens were aware of what was taking place. Wasn't anyone trying to help do something about it?

He said, "Yes, it is sad. But nothing can be done. You
don't understand the Abos. They are primitive, wild, bush
people. We have offered to educate them. Missionaries
have spent years trying to convert them. In the past they
were cannibals. Now they still do not want to turn loose
of their customs and old beliefs. Most prefer the hardship
of the desert. The Outback is hard country, but these are
the world's hardest people. Those who do straddle the
two cultures are rarely successful. It is true they are a
dying race. Their population is declining by their own free
will. They are hopelessly illiterate people with no ambition or drive for success. After two hundred years they
still don't fit in. What's more, they don't try. In business
they are unreliable and undependable—act like they can't
tell time. Believe me, there is nothing you can do to
inspire them."

A few days went by, but never without my thinking of
the dead young man. I began to discuss my concern with
a woman in the health-care profession who, like myself,
had a special project under way. Her work involved dealing with the elderly Aboriginal natives. She was docu-
menting wild plants, herbs, and flowers that might scien-
tifically be found to help prevent or treat illness. The
authorities on that sort of knowledge were the bush people. Their track record for longevity and low incidence of
degenerative disease spoke for itself. She confirmed that
little headway had been made in any true integration of
the races but was willing to help me if I wanted to try and

see what difference, if any, one more person could make.

We invited twenty-two young half-breed Aborigines to a meeting. She introduced me. That evening I talked about the free enterprise system of government and discussed an organization called Junior Achievement for underprivileged inner-city youth. The goal was to find a product the group could make. I agreed to teach them how to purchase raw material, organize a workforce, make the item, market it, and get established in the business and banking community. They were interested.

At the next meeting we talked about possible projects. My grandparents lived in Iowa during my youth. I remembered Grandma pushing up the window, taking out a little adjustable screen, stretching it to the width of the window as it rested on the sill, then pulling the pane back down. It gave about a foot of screened space. The house I was living in, typical of most older suburban houses in Australia, had no screens. Air conditioning was not common in residences, so the neighbors merely lifted their windows and let the winged creatures fly in and out. There were no mosquitoes, but we did have a daily battle with flying cockroaches. I went to bed alone but often awakened to find my pillow shared by several two-inch, black, hard-shelled insects. I felt the screen would be a shield against their encroachment.

The group agreed screens were a good item to launch the business. I knew a specific couple in the United States to contact for help. He was a design engineer at a large corporation, and she was an artist. If I could explain what I needed in a letter, I knew they could create a blueprint. It arrived two weeks later. My dear elderly Aunt Nola back in Iowa offered to lend financial support to buy the initial supplies and get us rolling. We required a place to work. Garages are rare, but carports are plentiful, so we acquired one and worked in the open air.

Each young Aborigine seemed to slip naturally into their most talented position. We had a bookkeeper, someone to shop for supplies, another who took pride in perfect calculations of our running inventory. We had specialists on each segment of production, even several natural-born sales representatives. I stood back and observed the company structure forming. It was apparent that, without my input on how to do it, they mutually agreed that the person who liked to do the cleaning up, the janitoral duties, was as valuable to the overall success of the project as the people who made the final sale. Our approach was to offer the screens free for a few days on a trial basis. When we returned, if the screens had been satisfactory, the party paid us. We usually got an order for the rest of the windows on the property. I also taught them the good old American concept of asking for referrals.

Time slipped by. My days were spent working, writing training material, traveling, teaching, and lecturing. Most evenings were spent enjoying the company of the young black people. The original group remained intact. Their bank account grew steadily, and we established trust funds for each one.

On a weekend date with Geoff, I explained our project and my desire to help the young people become financially independent. Maybe they wouldn't be hired to work for companies, but they couldn't be stopped from buying one if they accumulated enough wealth. I suppose I was boasting a little about my input into their budding sense of self-worth. Geoff said, "Goodonyou, Yank." But the next time we met he brought along some history books. Sitting on his patio overlooking the world's most beautiful harbor, I spent one Saturday afternoon reading.

History quoted Rev. George King in the *Australian Sunday Times,* on December 16, 1923, as saying, "The Aborigines of Australia constitute, no doubt, a low type in the scale of humanity. They possess no reliable traditional history of themselves, their doings, or origin; nor, if swept from the earth at the present time, would they leave behind them a single work of art as a memorial of their existence as a people; but they appear to have roamed over the vast plains of Australia at a very early period of the world's history."

There was another more current quote from John Burless regarding the attitude of white Australia: "I'll give you something, but you haven't anything that I would want."

Excerpts from ethnology and anthropology of the Fourteenth Congress of the Australian and New Zealand Association for the Advancement of Science said:

> The sense of smell is undeveloped.
> Memory is only slightly developed.
> Children are without any great willpower.
> They are inclined to be untruthful and cowardly.
> They do not suffer pain as acutely as do the higher
>   races.

Next came the history books that say an Australian Aboriginal boy becomes a man by having his penis split from scrotum to meatus by a dull stone knife, without anesthetic, without expression of pain. Adulthood is obtained while having a front tooth beaten from one's head by a holy man wielding a rock, it is having one's foreskin served as dinner to male relatives, and being sent into the desert alone, terrified and bleeding, to prove one can survive. History also says they were cannibals and that the women sometimes ate their own babies, relishing the most tender parts. One story in the book tells of two brothers: The younger one stabbed his older brother in a dispute over a woman. After amputating his own gangrened leg, the older brother blinded the younger one, and they lived happily ever after. One walked along on a kangaroo prosthesis, leading the other at the end of a long pole. The information was gruesome, but the most impossible to comprehend was a government information pamphlet about the primitive surgery that states the Aborigines fortunately have a less-than-human threshold of pain.

My project companions were not savages. If anything they were comparable to the disadvantaged youth at home. They lived in isolated sections of the community; over half the families were on the dole. It appeared to me they had settled for a life of secondhand Levis, a tin of hot beer, and one individual every few years who made it big.

The following Monday, back with the screen-making project, I realized I was witnessing genuine noncompetitive support, alien to my business world. It was truly refreshing.

I asked the young employees about their heritage. They told me tribal significance had been lost long ago. A few remembered grandparents telling about life when the Aboriginal race alone inhabited the continent. Then there were tribes of saltwater people, and Emu people, among others; but quite truthfully, they did not want to be reminded of their dark skin and the difference it represented. They hoped to marry someone of lighter color and eventually for their children to blend in.

Our company was by all standards very successful, so I was not surprised one day when I received a phone call inviting me to a meeting that was being held by a tribe of Aborigines across the continent. The call implied it was not just a meeting, it was *my* meeting. "Please make arrangements to attend," the native voice requested.

I went shopping for new clothes, purchased a round-trip flight, and made hotel reservations. I told the people I was working with that I would be gone for a while and explained the unique summons. I shared my excitement with Geoff, my landlady, and in a letter to my daughter. It was an honor that people so far away had heard of our project and wanted to express their appreciation.

"Transportation from the hotel to the meeting will be provided," I was told. They were to pick me up at noon. Obviously that meant it was an award luncheon. I wondered what sort of menu would be served.

Well, Ooota had been there promptly at twelve o'clock, but the question of what Aborigines serve for food still remained unanswered.

6

THE BANQUET

THE INCREDIBLE healing oil mixture, made by heating leaves and removing the oil residue, was working—my feet finally felt relieved enough that courage to stand once again entered my thoughts. Off to my right was a group of women who seemed to have an assembly-line project under way. They were gathering large leaves; while one woman poked into the brush and dead trees with a long digging stick, another removed a handful of something and put it on the leaf. Then a second leaf topped the contents and was folded so the final package was given to a runner who in turn took it to the fire and buried it in the coals. I was curious. This was our first meal together, the menu I had wondered about for weeks. I hobbled over for a closer view and could not believe my eyes. The scooped hand held a large, white, crawling worm.

I took another deep sigh. I had lost track of the number of times today I had been left speechless. One thing was for certain. I knew I would never be so hungry I would eat a worm! At that moment, however, I was learning a lesson. Never say "never." To this day it is a word I have tried to eliminate from my vocabulary. I have learned there are things I prefer, and others I avoid, but the word *never* leaves no room for unseen situations, and *never* covers a long, long time.

Evenings were a real joy with the tribal people. They told stories, sang, danced, played games, had heart-to-heart chats. This was a real time of sharing. There was always some activity while we waited for the food to be prepared. They did a lot of massaging and rubbing of each other's shoulders, backs, even their scalps. I saw them manipulating necks and spines. Later in the journey we exchanged techniques—I taught them the American method of adjusting the back and other joints; they taught me theirs.

That first day, I did not see any cups, plates, or serving bowls unpacked. I had guessed correctly. This was to remain an informal atmosphere with all meals eaten in picnic style. It wasn't long before the folded-leaf casseroles were removed from the charcoals. Mine was handled with the devotion of a special-duty nurse. I watched everyone open theirs, and eat the contents with their fingers. My hand-held banquet was warm but there was no movement, so I became brave enough to look inside. The grub worm had disappeared. At least it didn't look like a worm any longer. It was now a brown, crumbled bed, resembling roasted peanuts or pork rind. I thought to myself, "I think I can handle this." I did, and it tasted good! I did not know that cooking, certainly cooking things beyond recognition, was being done for me and was not a common practice.

That night it was explained to me that my work with the urban-dwelling Aborigines had been reported. Even though these young adults were not full-blooded natives and did not belong to this tribe, my work was a display of someone who truly seemed to care. The summons came because it appeared to them I was crying for help. I was found to have pure intent. The problem was that, as they saw it, I did not understand the Aboriginal culture, and certainly not the code of this tribe. The ceremonies performed earlier in the day were tests. I was found acceptable and worthy of learning the knowledge of the true relationship of humans to the world we live in, the world beyond, the dimension from which we came, and the dimension where we shall all return. I was going to be exposed to the understanding of my own beingness.

As I sat, my soothed feet now encased in their precious and limited supply of leaves, Ooota explained what a tremendous undertaking it was for these desert nomads to walk with me. I was being allowed to share their life. Never before had they associated with a white person or even considered any kind of relationship with one. In fact, they had avoided it for all time. According to them, every other tribe in Australia had submitted to the rule of the white government. They were the last of the holdouts. They usually traveled in small families of six to ten people but had come together for this event.

Ooota said something to the group, and each person said something to me. They were telling me their names. The words were very difficult for me, but luckily their names meant something. Names are not used in the same way that we would use "Debbie" or "Cody" in the United States, so I could relate each person to the meaning of the name, instead of trying to pronounce the word itself. Each child is named at birth, but it is understood that as a person develops, the birth name will be outgrown, and the individuals will select for themselves a more appropriate greeting. Hopefully, one's name will change several times in a lifetime as wisdom, creativity, and purpose also become more clearly defined with time. Our group contained Story Teller, Tool Maker, Secret Keeper, Sewing Master, and Big Music, among many others.

At last Ooota pointed to me and spoke to each person, pronouncing the same word repeatedly. I thought they were trying to say my first name but then decided they were instead going to call me by my last name. It wasn't either. The word they used that night, and the name I continued to carry for the journey, was *Mutant*. I did not understand why Ooota, who was spokesperson for both languages, was teaching them to say such a strange term. Mutant, to me, meant some significant change in basic structure, resulting in a form of mutation and no longer like the original. But actually it didn't really matter, for at that point, my whole day, my whole life was in total confusion.

Ooota said in some Aboriginal nations they only used about eight names total—more like a numbering system. Everyone of the same generation and same sex were considered the same relation, so everyone had several mothers, fathers, brothers, etc.

As darkness approached, I asked about the acceptable method of relieving oneself. Then I wished I had paid closer attention to my daughter's cat, Zuke, because our bathroom facilities consisted of walking out into the desert, digging a hole in the sand, squatting, and covering the contents with more sand. I was cautioned to watch for snakes. They become most active after the hottest portion of the day is over, but before the cool of night. I had visions of wicked eyes and poisonous tongues in the sand being awakened by my action. When I traveled through Europe I had complained about the dreadful toilet paper. For South America I had packed my own. Here the absence of paper was the least of my concerns.

When I returned to the group from my desert venture, we shared in a communal bag of Aboriginal stone tea. It was made by dropping hot rocks into a container of precious water. The container had originally served as bladder for some animal. Wild herbs were added to the heated water and left to steep toward perfection. We passed the unique vessel around the group back and forth. It tasted wonderful!

The tribal stone tea, I found, was saved for special circumstances, such as my novice completion of the first day's walk. They realized the difficulty I would experience without shoes, shade, or transportation. The herbs added to the water to form the tea were not intended to add variety to the menu, nor were they subtle medication or nourishment. They were a celebration, a way of recognizing the group accomplishment. I did not give up, demand to be returned to the city, nor did I cry out. Their Aboriginal spirit was being received, they felt, by me.

The people then began to smooth out places in the sand, and each took from the common bundle carried earlier a round roll of hide or skin. An older woman had been staring at me all evening with an uncommitted expression on her face. "What is she thinking?" I asked

Ooota. "That you have lost your smell of flowers and that you are probably from outer space." I smiled, and with that she handed me my pack. Her name was Sewing Master.

"It is dingo," Ooota advised. I knew the dingo was Australia's wild dog, similar to our coyote or wolf. "It's very versatile. You can put it under you on the ground, or cover yourself or comfort your head."

"Great," I thought. "I can select which twenty-four inches of my body I want to comfort!"

I elected to use it between me and the crawling creatures I envisioned nearby. It had been years since I had slept on the ground. As a child, I recalled spending time on a big flat rock in the Mojave Desert of California. We lived in Barstow. The main attraction was a big mound called "B" hill. Many a summer day I took a bottle of orange Nehi drink and a peanut-butter sandwich and hiked up and around the hill. I always ate on the same flat rock and then spent time on my back looking up at the clouds and finding objects in them. Childhood seemed a long time ago. Funny how the sky remained the same. Guess I hadn't paid much attention to celestial bodies over the years. Above was a cobalt canopy speckled with silver. I could clearly see the pattern that is depicted on the Australian flag referred to as the Southern Cross.

As I lay there I thought about my adventure. How would I ever describe what happened today? A door had opened, and I had entered a world I didn't know existed. It certainly was not a life of luxury. I had lived in different places and traveled to many countries, on all forms of transportation, but never anything like this. I guessed it was going to be okay after all.

I would explain to them the next morning that one day was all I really required to appreciate their culture. My feet would endure the journey back to the jeep. Maybe I could take some of their great foot balm with me, because it had really helped. A sample of this lifestyle would be sufficient for me. But today hadn't been that bad, excluding my tortured feet.

Someplace down deep I was really grateful for learning more about how other people live. I was beginning to see that more than blood passes through the human heart. I closed my eyes and said a silent "thank you" to the Power above.

Someone at the far side of the camp said something. It was repeated by first one and then another. They were passing it along, each one saying the same phrase, crisscrossing from one reclining figure to another. Finally the phrase was given to Ooota, whose sleeping mat was nearest to mine. He turned and said: "You are welcome; this day is good."

Somewhat startled at their answer to my unvoiced words, I responded by saying my "thank you" and "you're welcome" the second time aloud.

7

WHAT IS SOCIAL SECURITY?

I WAS awakened in the morning before any exposure to sun rays by the noise from people gathering up the few scattered articles we had used the evening before. I was told the days gained in heat, so we would walk during the cooler morning hours, rest, and then resume our journey into the later night. I folded the dingo hide and handed it to a man who was packing. The hides were left easily accessible, because during the peak heat of the day, we would find shelter, build a *wiltja,* or temporary brush shelter, or use our sleeping skins to construct shade.

Most of the animals do not like the glaring sun. Only the lizards, spiders, and bush flies are alert and active at one hundred plus degrees. Even snakes must bury themselves in the extreme heat, or they become dehydrated and die. It is hard sometimes to spot snakes as they hear us coming and peek their heads out of the sandy soil to find the source of the vibration. I am grateful that at the time I was not aware there are two hundred different types of snakes in Australia, and more than seventy are poisonous.

I did learn that day, however, the remarkable relationship the Aborigines have with nature. Before we started walking for the day, we formed a close-knit semicircle, all of us facing the east. The Tribal Elder moved to the center and started chanting. A beat was established and carried through by each person clapping their hands, stomping their feet, or hitting their thighs. It lasted about fifteen minutes. This was routine each morning, and I discovered that it was a very important part of our life together. It was morning (prayer, centering, goal setting, whatever you want to call it). These people believe everything exists on the planet for a reason. Everything has a purpose. There are no freaks, misfits, or accidents. There are only misunderstandings and mysteries not yet revealed to mortal man.

The purpose of the plant kingdom is to feed animals and humans, to hold the soil together, to enhance beauty, to balance the atmosphere. I was told the plants and trees sing to us humans silently, and all they ask in return is for us to sing to them. My scientific mind immediately translated this to mean nature's oxygen–carbon dioxide exchange. The primary purpose of the animal is not to feed humans, but it agrees to that when necessary. It is to balance the atmosphere, and be a companion and teacher by example. So each morning the tribe sends out a thought or message to the animals and plants in front of us. They say, "We are walking your way. We are coming to honor your purpose for existence." It is up to the plants and animals to make their own arrangements about who will be chosen.

The Real People tribe never go without food. Always, the universe responds to their mind-talk. They believe the world is a place of abundance. Just as you and I might gather to listen to someone play the piano, and honor that talent and purpose, they sincerely do the same thing with everything in nature. When a snake appeared on our path, it was obviously there to provide our dinner. The daily food was a very important part of our evening celebration. I learned that the appearance of food was not taken for granted. It was first requested, always expected to appear, and did appear, but was gratefully received and genuine gratitude was always given. The tribe begins each day by saying thank you to Oneness for the day, for themselves, their friends, and the world. They sometimes ask for specifics, but it is always phrased "If it is in my highest good and the highest good for all life everywhere."

After the morning semicircle gathering, I tried to tell Ooota it was time for him to take me back to the jeep, but it seemed he was nowhere in sight. Finally, I acknowledged I could endure one more day.

The tribe carried no provisions. They planted no crops; they participated in no harvest. They walked the blazing Australian Outback, knowing each day they would receive bountiful blessings of the universe. The universe never disappointed them.

We ate no breakfast the first day, and I found that to be the usual pattern. Sometimes our meal was at night; however, we ate whenever the food appeared, regardless of the position of the sun. Many times we ate a bite here and there, not a meal as we know it.

We carried several bladder water vessels. I know that humans are approximately 70 percent water and require a minimum of one gallon per day under ideal conditions. Observing the Aborigines, I saw they did require much less, and drank less than I. In fact, they rarely drank from the water containers. Their bodies seemed to use the moisture in food to a maximum. They believe Mutants have many addictions, and water is included.

We used the water to soak what appeared to be dead and dried-out weeds at mealtime. The brown stubs went into the water as lifeless, dehydrated sticks and came out many times miraculously looking like fresh celery stalks.

They could find water where there was absolutely no appearance of moisture. Sometimes they would lie down on the sand and hear water underneath or hold their hands with the palm down and scan the ground for water. They put long hollow reeds into the earth, sucked on the end, and created a minifountain. The water was sandy and a dark color but tasted pure and refreshing. They were aware of water in the distance by watching the heat vapors and could even smell and feel it in the breeze. I now understand why so many people who try to explore the inner regions die so quickly. It would take the native expertise to survive.

When we took water from a rocky crevice, I was taught how to approach the area so I did not contaminate it with my human scent and frighten the animals. After all, it was their water too. The animals had as much right to it as people. The tribe never took all the water, regardless of how low our supply was at the moment. At any water area, the people used the same spot from which to drink. Each type of animal seemed to follow the pattern. Only the birds disregarded the access rule and felt at home drinking, splashing, and excreting freely.

The tribal members could look at the ground and tell what creatures were nearby. As children they learn the habit of minute observation and so recognize at a glance the sort of marks that are present upon the sand from walking, hopping, or crawling creatures. They are so accustomed to seeing each others' footprints that they not only can identify the party but can tell from the length of the stride if the person is feeling well or walking slowly from illness. The slightest deviation in the footprint can tell them the most probable destination of the walker. Their perception is developed well beyond the limitations of people growing up in other cultures. Their senses of hearing, sight, and smell seem to be on superhuman levels. Footprints have vibrations that tell much more than merely what one sees on the sand.

I learned later that Aboriginal trackers have been known to tell from tire marks the speed, type of vehicle, date and time, and even the number of passengers.

Over the next few days, we ate bulbs, tubers, and other vegetables that grew underground, similar to potatoes and yams. They could locate a plant ready to harvest without pulling it out of the ground. They would move their hands over the plants and comment: "This one is growing, but not ready yet," or "Yes, this one is prepared to give birth." All the stalks looked the same to me, so after disturbing several and watching them be replanted, I found it best to wait until I was told what to pull up. They explained it as the natural dowsing ability given to all humans. Because my society did not encourage listening to one's intuitive direction, and even frowned on it as being supernatural, possibly evil, I had to be trained to learn what comes naturally. Ultimately they taught me to dowse by asking plants if they were ready to be honored for their purpose of being. I asked permission from the universe and then scanned with the palm of my hand. Sometimes I felt heat, and sometimes my fingers seemed to have an uncontrollable twitch when I was over ripe vegetation. When I learned to do it, I could sense a giant step forward in my acceptance from the tribal members. It seemed to signify I was a little less mutated and perhaps becoming gradually more real.

It was important that we never used an entire bed of any plant. Enough was always left for new growth. The tribal people are amazingly aware of what they called the song or unvoiced sounds of the soil. They can sense input from the environment, do something unique in decoding it, and then consciously act, almost as if they had developed some tiny celestial receiver that universal messages came through.

On one of the first days we walked over a dry lake bed. There were irregular, wide breaks in the surface, and each piece seemed to have curled edges. Several of the women gathered the white clay, and later it was pulverized into fine powder for paint.

The women carried long sticks and dug them into the hard clay surface. Several feet below, they found moisture and extracted little round mud balls. To my surprise, the globs, when rubbed free of the dirt, were actually frogs. They apparently survive the dehydrating condition by burying themselves several feet below the surface. After being roasted they were still quite moist and tasted like chicken breast. Over the next months we had an array of food appear before us to be honored as our daily celebration of universal life. We ate kangaroo, wild horse, lizards, snakes, bugs, grub worms of all sizes and colors, ants, termites, anteaters, birds, fish, seeds, nuts, fruit, plants too numerous to mention, and even crocodile.

On the first morning, one of the women came to me. She took the filthy twine from her head and, holding my long hair up off my neck, used it to secure a new upswept hair fashion. Her name was Spirit Woman. I didn't understand to what she was spiritually related, but after we became good friends, I decided it was to me.

I lost track of days, weeks, of time itself. I gave up trying to ask about returning to the jeep. It seemed futile, and something else appeared to be taking place. They had some plan in mind. It was apparent, however, that at this time I was not being allowed to know what it was. Tests of my strength, my reactions, my beliefs, were continually challenged, but why, I did not know, and I questioned if people who do not read or write have another method for student report cards.

Some days the sand became so hot I could literally hear my feet! They sizzled, like hamburgers frying in a pan. As the blisters dried and hardened, a sort of hoof began to form.

As time went by, my physical stamina reached amazing new heights. Without any food to eat at breakfast or lunch, I learned to nourish myself on the view. I watched lizard races, insects grooming themselves, and found hidden pictures in stone and sky.

The people pointed out sacred places in the desert. It seemed everything was sacred: clumps of rocks, hills, ravines, even smooth dry basins. There seem to be invisible lines that mark the home territory of former tribes. They demonstrated how they measure distance by singing songs in very specific details and rhythms. Some songs might have one hundred verses. Every word and every pause must be exact. There could be no ad-lib or lapse in memory because it is literally a measuring stick. They actually sang us from one location to another. I could only compare these song lines to a method of measurement developed by a friend of mine who is sightless. They have refused a written language because to them that gives away the power of memory. If you practice and demand recall, you retain optimum level performance.

The sky remained a cloudless pastel blue, day after day, with only a complex of hues for variety. The bright light of midday bounced off the glistening sand to strain and yet strengthen my eyes which became renewed inlets for a river of vision.

I began to appreciate, not take for granted, the ability of renewal after a night's sleep, how a few sips of water could truly quench my thirst, and the whole range of tastes from sweet to bitter. I had spent my life being reminded of job security, the necessity of acquiring a hedge against inflation, buying real estate, and saving for my retirement. Out here our only security was the never-failing cycle of morning dawn and setting sun. It amazed me that the world's most insecure race, according to my standards, suffered no ulcers, hypertension, or cardiovascular disease.

I began to see beauty and the oneness of all life in the strangest sights. A den of snakes, perhaps two hundred in all, each the circumference of my thumb, wove in and out like a moving pattern along the side of an ornate museum vase. I have always hated snakes. But I was seeing them as necessary for the balance of nature, as necessary for the survival of our group of travelers, as creatures so difficult to accept lovingly that they have become objects to include in art and religion. I could not conceive of looking forward to eating smoked snake meat let alone raw snake, but there came a time when I actually did. I learned how precious the moisture of any food can be.

Over the months, we encountered extremes in weather. The first night I used my allotted skin as a mattress, but when the cold nights set in, it got transferred to a blanket. Most of the people lay on the bare ground cuddled in someone's arms. They depended on warmth from another body rather than the nearby fire. On the coldest nights, numerous fires were made. In the past they had traveled with domesticated dingos that provided help in hunting, companionship, and warmth on cold nights, hence the colloquialism "three-dog night."

Several evenings we would lie on the ground in a unique circular pattern. It made better use of our coverings, and the cluster seemed to preserve and transfer body heat more efficiently. We dug slots in the sand and put a layer of hot coals down, then some additional sand on top. Half the skins were placed under us, and half over us. Two people shared each slotted space. All our feet were joined in the center.

I remember propping my chin on both hands and looking into the vast expanse of sky overhead. I felt the essence of these wonderful, pure, innocent, loving people surrounding me. This circle of souls in the daisy pattern, with tiny fires between each group of two bodies, must have been a wonderful sight if it were observed from the cosmos above.

They appeared to be touching only each other's toes,

but I was learning day by day how their consciousness had been for all time touching the universal consciousness of humankind.

It was beginning to register why they so sincerely felt I was a Mutant, and I was equally sincere in my gratitude for the opportunity to awaken.

8

~~~~~~~~~~~~~~~~~~~~~~~~~~

CORDLESS PHONE

THIS DAY started relatively the same as the preceding ones, so I had no idea what was in store. We did have breakfast, which was not common. The previous day we had come upon a grinding stone on our path. It was a large, very heavy, oval-shaped rock—obviously too much of a burden to carry—left in the open for the use of any traveler fortunate enough to have seeds or grain. The women transformed plant stalks into a fine meal, and this mixed with salt grass and water formed flat cakes. They resembled undersized pancakes.

We faced east in our morning prayer service and gave thanks for all our blessings. We sent our daily message out to the food kingdom.

One of the younger men took a turn in the center. It was explained he had offered to perform a special task that day. He left camp early and ran on ahead. We had walked several hours when the Elder stopped and fell to his knees. Everyone gathered around as he remained in the kneeling position, his arms held out in front, gently swaying. I asked Ooota what was happening. He motioned for me to remain quiet. No one was saying anything but all their faces were intent. Finally, Ooota turned to me and said the young scout who had left us earlier was sending in a message. He was asking permission to cut off the tail of a kangaroo he had killed.

It finally dawned on me why it was quiet every day as we walked. These people used mental telepathy to communicate most of the time. I was witnessing it. There was absolutely no sound to be heard, but messages were being relayed between people twenty miles apart.

"Why does he want to remove the tail?" I asked.

"Because it is the heaviest part of the kangaroo, and he is too ill to carry the animal comfortably. It is taller than he is, and he is telling us that the water he stopped to drink was foul and has caused his body to become too hot. He has beads of fluid coming from his face."

A silent telepathic reply was sent. Ooota advised me we would stop for the day. The people began to dig a pit in preparation for the large meat we would be receiving. Others began preparing herbal medication under the instructions of Medicine Man and Female Healer.

Several hours later, into our camp walked the young man, carrying the huge gutted kangaroo minus a tail. The roo had been disemboweled, and the opening was pinned shut by sharpened sticks. The entrails now served as rope holding the four legs together. He had carried the one hundred pounds of meat on his head and shoulders. The fellow was perspiring and obviously ill. I watched as the tribe went into action dealing with the healing, and the cooking of our meal.

First the kangaroo was held over a flaming fire; the smell of burning fur hung in the air like a Los Angeles smog. The head was cut off and legs broken so the sinew could be removed. The body was lowered into the pit which contained glowing coals on all sides. A small container of water was placed in one corner of the deep hole and a long reed protruded upward. More brush was piled on top. From time to time over the next few hours, the primary chef would lean through the smoke, blow into the long reed, and force water to be released below the surface. The steam was immediately apparent.

At serving time only the outer few inches were roasted; the rest oozed in blood. I told them I just had to put my portion on a stick in hot-dog fashion and cook it. No problem! They quickly prepared an appropriate fork.

Meanwhile, the young hunter was receiving medical attention. First he was given an herbal drink. Next, using cool sand extracted from a deep hole they had just dug, his attendants packed it around his feet. I was told that if they could draw the heat from his head downward, it would balance his overall body temperature. It sounded very strange to me, but it did indeed reduce the fever. The herbs also were effective in preventing the stomach pain and loose bowels I expected to observe from such an ordeal.

It was really remarkable. If I had not witnessed it myself, it would have been hard to believe, especially the communicating by telepathy. I told Ooota how I felt.

He smiled and said, "Now you know how it feels to a native the first time they go into the city and see you put a coin into the phone, dial a number, and start talking to your relative. The native thinks that is incredible."

"Yes," I replied. "Both ways are good, but yours sure works best out here where we have no quarters and no phone booths."

Mental telepathy was something I sensed the people back home would find difficult to believe. They could easily accept that humans around the world were cruel to each other, but would be reluctant to believe there were people on earth who are not racist, who live together in total support and harmony, who discover their own unique talent and honor it as well as honor everyone else. The reason, according to Ooota, that Real People can use telepathy is because above all they never tell a lie, not a small fabrication, not a partial truth, nor any gross unreal statement. No lies at all, so they have nothing to hide. They are a group of people who are not afraid to have their minds open to receive and are willing to give one another information. Ooota explained how it worked. If at the age of two, for instance, one child saw another playing with some toy—a rock perhaps being pulled by a string—if that child went to take the other's toy, immediately he would feel all the adult eyes turned his way. He would learn that his intent of taking without permission was known and not acceptable. The second child would also learn to share, to learn nonattachment to objects. That child had already enjoyed and stored the memory of fun, so it is the emotion of happiness that is desired, not the object.

Mental telepathy—it is the way humans were designed to communicate. Different languages and various written alphabets are eliminated as obstacles when people use head-to-head talk. But it would never work in my world, I reasoned, where people steal from the company, cheat on taxes, have affairs. My people would never stand for being literally "open-minded." There is too much deception, too much hurt, too much bitterness to hide.

But for myself, could I personally forgive everybody whom I believed had wronged me? Could I forgive myself for all the hurts I had inflicted? Someday I hoped to be able to lay my mind out on a table, like the Aborigines, and stand by as my motives were exposed and examined.

The Real People don't think the voice was designed for talking. You do that with your heart/head center. If the voice is used for speech, one tends to get into small, unnecessary, and less spiritual conversation. The voice is made for singing, for celebration, and healing.

They told me everyone has multiple talents and everyone can sing. If I don't honor the gift because I thought I couldn't sing, that wouldn't diminish the singer within me.

Later during our journey, when they worked with me to develop my mental communication, I learned that as long as I had anything in my heart or my head I still felt necessary to hide, it would not work. I had to come to peace with *everything*.

I had to learn to forgive myself, not to judge, but to learn from the past. They showed me how vital it is to accept, be truthful, and love myself so I could do the same with others.

9

HAT FOR THE OUTBACK

THE BUSH flies in the Outback are horrendous. The hordes appear with the first rays of sunlight. They infest the sky, traveling in black packs of what seems to be millions. It looked and sounded like a Kansas funnel tornado.

I could not help eating and breathing flies. They crawled into my ears, up my nose, clawed my eyes, and even managed to get past my teeth and enter my throat. They had a disgusting sweet taste as I gagged and choked. They clung to my body so when I looked down, it appeared I was wearing some sort of black moving armor. They didn't bite, but I was too busy suffering to notice. They were so big, and so quick, and there were so many of them, it was almost unbearable. My eyes suffered the most.

The tribal people have a sense of where and when the flies will appear. When they see or hear the insects approaching, they immediately stop, close their eyes, and stand still, arms hanging limply at the side.

I was learning from them to look at the positive side of virtually everything we encountered, but the flies would have been my downfall if I had not been rescued. In fact, it was the most grueling ordeal I have ever suffered. I could well understand how being covered with millions of moving insect legs could drive a person insane. I was just lucky that I didn't snap.

One morning, I was approached by a committee of three women. They came to me and asked for strands of my hair, which they plucked. I have bleached my hair for thirty years, so when I entered the desert it was a soft beige color. It was long, but I always wore it pulled up. Over the weeks of our walking, without it ever being washed, brushed, or even combed, I did not know what it looked like. We hadn't even seen a surface of water clear or still enough in which to see a reflection. I could only envision a matted, tangled, filthy mess. I wore the headband Spirit Woman had given me to keep it out of my eyes.

The women got sidetracked from their project when they discovered that under my blond hair I was growing dark roots. They ran and reported it to the Elder. He was middle-aged, quiet, and had a very strong, almost athletic build. In the short time we had traveled together, I had observed how sincerely he talked with members and thanked each one without hesitation for help they had provided to the group. I could well understand why he was in the place of leadership.

He reminded me of someone else. Years before, I had been standing in the lobby of Southwestern Bell in St. Louis. It was about seven A.M. The janitor, who was busy scouring the marble floor, had admitted me so I could wait indoors out of the rain. An elongated black car pulled up and the president of Texas Bell walked in. He nodded to me, acknowledging my presence, and said "Good morning" to the cleaning man. Then he told the man how much he appreciated his dedication, and that no matter what person came into that building, even the highest officials of our government, he could always be confident it would sparkle because of this employee. I knew he wasn't blowing hot air; he was very sincere. I was just a bystander, yet I could feel the pride radiating from that janitor's face. I learned there is something about true leaders that transcends boundaries. My father used to tell me, "People don't work for a company. They work for other people." I could see executive leadership characteristics in the actions of the Outback Tribal Elder.

After he came to witness the strange spectacle of the blond-haired Mutant with dark brown roots, he allowed all the others a chance to see the wonder. Their eyes seemed to light up, and each one smiled in pleasure. Ooota explained that it was because they felt I was becoming more Aboriginal.

After the fun was over, the committee started back on their project, weaving together my hair strands with seeds, small bones, pods, some grass and the tendon from a kangaroo. When they finished, I was crowned with the most elaborate headband I had ever seen. All around it, hanging down to chin level, were long strands holding the woven objects. They explained that the Australian fishing hats with cork floaters, commonly used by sportsmen, were patterned after this ancient native idea of protection against the flies.

We did indeed encounter a horde of bush flies later

that very day, and my seeded headdress became a literal godsend.

Another day, when we were plagued by a deluge of flying and biting insects, they anointed me with snake oil and ashes from our campfire and had me roll in the sand. That combination discouraged the little critters. It was worth it to walk with an encrusted clown appearance, but flies crawling down into my ears and feeling an insect moving around inside my head was still an experience bordering on hell.

I asked several people how they could just stand there forever, limp, and let insects crawl over them. They merely smiled at me. Then I was told that the leader Regal Black Swan wanted to speak to me. "Do you understand how long forever is?" he asked. "It is a very, very long time. Eternity. We know in your society you wear time on your arm and do things on a schedule, so I ask, do you understand how long forever is?"

"Yes," I said. "I understand forever."

"Good," he replied. "Then we can tell you something more. Everything in Oneness has a purpose. There are no freaks, misfits, or accidents. There are only things that humans do not understand. You believe the bush flies to be bad, to be hell, and so for you they are, but it is only because you are minus the necessary understanding and wisdom. In truth, they are necessary and beneficial creatures. They crawl down our ears and clean out the wax and sand that we get from sleeping each night. Do you see we have perfect hearing? Yes, they climb up our nose and clean it out too." He pointed to my nose and said, "You have very small holes, not a big koala nose as we have. It is going to get much hotter in the days to come and you will suffer if you do not have a clean nose. In extreme heat you must not open your mouth to the air. Of all people who need a clean nose, it is you. The flies crawl and cling to our body and take off everything that is eliminated." He held out his arm as he said, "See how soft and smooth our skin is, and look at yours. We have never known a person who changed colors merely by walking. You came to us one color, then became bright red, now you are drying and falling away. You are becoming smaller and smaller each day. We have never known anyone who left their skin on the sand as a snake does. You need the flies to clean your skin, and someday we will come to the place where the flies have laid the larva and again we will be provided with a meal." He took a deep sigh as he looked at me intently and said, "Humans cannot exist if everything that is unpleasant is eliminated instead of understood. When the flies come, we surrender. Perhaps you are ready to do the same."

The next time I heard bush flies in the distance I untied my headband from my waist and studied it but decided I could do as my companions suggested. So the flies came and I left. I went to New York in my mind. I went to a very expensive health spa. With my eyes closed I felt someone cleaning out my ears and nose. I pictured this trained technician's diploma hanging on the wall above me. I felt hundreds of tiny cotton balls cleaning my entire body. Finally the creatures left, and I returned mentally back to the Outback. It was true, surrender is definitely the correct answer in certain circumstances.

I wondered what else in my life I perceived to be wrong or difficult instead of exploring to understand the true purpose.

Having no mirror all this time seemed to have an impact on my awareness. It was like walking around inside a capsule with eyeholes. I was always looking out, looking at others, observing how they were relating to what I was doing or what I was saying. For the first time, it seemed my life was totally honest. I wasn't wearing certain clothing as I was expected to do in the business world. I had no makeup. My nose had peeled a dozen times by now. There was no pretense—no ego fighting for attention. In the group there was no gossip or anyone trying to out-maneuver someone else.

Without a mirror to frighten me back into reality, I could experience feeling beautiful. Obviously I wasn't, but I felt beautiful. The people accepted me as I was. They made me feel included, and unique, and wonderful. I was learning how it felt to be in a state of unconditional acceptance.

I went to sleep on the sand mattress with a deeply embedded childhood verse from Snow White echoing in my head:

Mirror, mirror on the wall
Who is the fairest one of all?

10

JEWELRY

THE FURTHER we walked, the hotter it got. The hotter it got, the more vegetation and all life seemed to disappear. We were walking in a terrain of basically sand with a few tall, dried, dead stalks appearing in clumps. There was nothing in the distance—no mountains, no trees, nothing. It was a day of sand, sand, and sandy weeds.

That day, we began carrying a fire stick. It is a piece of wood kept glowing by swinging it gently. In the desert, where vegetation is so treasured, each tiny trick found to insure survival is utilized. The fire stick was used to ignite the night's campfire when dry grass became a premium. I also observed tribal members collecting the rare piles of dung left by desert creatures, especially those of the dingos. It proved to be powerful, odorless fuel.

Everyone is multitalented, I was reminded. These people spend their life exploring themselves as musician, healer, cook, storyteller, and so on, and giving themselves new names and promotions. I started my first tribal participation into exploring my talents by referring to myself in a joking manner as Dung Collector.

That day, a lovely young girl walked into the weed patch and magically emerged carrying a beautiful yellow flower on a long stalk. She tied the stem around her neck so the flower was dangling in front like a costly piece of jewelry. The members gathered around her and told her how lovely she looked and what a wonderful selection she had made. All day she received the compliments. I could sense her glow from feeling especially pretty that day.

Watching her, I was reminded of an incident that happened in my office just before leaving the United States. A patient came to me who was suffering from severe stress syndrome. When I asked her what was going on in her life, she told me the insurance company had raised the rates on one of her diamond necklaces another eight hundred dollars. She had found someone in New York City who claimed he could make an exact duplicate of her necklace using imitation stones. She was going to fly there, stay while it was completed, and then return to put her diamonds in a bank vault. This would not eliminate a large insurance fee, nor the need for it, because even in the best bank vault there is no guarantee of absolute safety, but the rate would be greatly reduced.

I remember asking about an annual civic ball coming up soon, and she said the imitation would be ready by then, so she would wear it.

At the end of our desert day, the girl of the Real People tribe laid the flower on the ground and returned it to Mother Earth. It had served its purpose. She was very grateful and had stored the memory of all her attention that day. It was confirmation that she was an attractive person. But she held no attachments to the item involved. It would wither and die and return to become humus and be recycled again.

I thought of the patient back home. Then I looked at the Aboriginal girl. Her jewelry had meaning, ours had financial value.

Truly, someone in this world had their value system in the wrong place, I concluded, but I didn't think it was these primitive people here, in the so called never-never land of Australia.

11

GRAVY

THE AIR was so still, I could feel the hair growing in my armpits. I could also feel the callouses on the bottom of my feet becoming thicker as the deeper layers of skin dried.

Our walk came to an abrupt halt. We paused where two crossed sticks had once marked a grave. The monument no longer stood upright; the binding had rotted. Now, on the ground were merely two old twigs, one long, one short. Tool Maker picked up the lumber and removed a thin strip of hide from his dilly bag. Wrapping the animal tissue with professional precision, he reconstructed the cross. Several people picked up large rocks scattered nearby and placed them in an oval on the sand. The grave marker was then anchored to the earth. "Is this a tribal grave?" I asked Ooota.

"No," he answered. "It housed a Mutant. It has been here many, many years—long forgotten by your people and possibly even by the survivor who created it."

"Why then did you fix it?" I inquired.

"Why not? We do not understand, agree, or accept your ways, but we do not judge. We honor your position. You are where you are supposed to be, given your past choices and your current free will to make decisions. This place serves for us the same as other sacred sites. It is a time to pause, to reflect, to confirm our relationship to Divine Oneness and all life. There's nothing left here, you see, not even any bones! But my nation respects your nation. We bless it, release it, and become better beings for having passed this way."

That afternoon, I thought about reflection—looking at myself, sifting through the rubble of my past. It was dirty work, scary, and even dangerous. There were lots of old habits and old beliefs that I had defended with swords of vested interest. Would I have stopped to repair a Jewish or Buddhist grave? I could remember becoming upset in a traffic jam caused by people leaving a religious temple. Would I now have the understanding to remain centered, be nonjudgmental and let others follow their own path with my blessing? I was beginning to understand: we automatically give to each person we meet, but we choose what we give. Our words, our actions, must consciously set the stage for the life we wish to lead.

Suddenly there was a gust of wind. The air licked my body, scratching, like a cat's tongue on my already abused skin. It lasted only a few seconds, but somehow I knew that honoring traditions and values I did not understand, and did not agree with, was not going to be easy but would bring me immense benefits.

That night, as a full moon dominated the sky, we gathered around the outdoor hearth. An orange glow painted our faces as the conversation drifted onto the subject of food. It was an open dialogue. They asked me, and I answered everything I possibly could. They listened to my every word. I told them about apples, how we created hybrid varieties, made applesauce, and Mom's "good-ole" apple pie. They promised to find wild apples for me to sample. I learned that the Real People were fundamentally vegetarians. For centuries they freely ate the natural wild fruits, yams, berries, nuts, and seeds. They occasionally added fish and eggs when such an item presented itself with the purpose for being, to become part of the Aborigine's body. They prefer not to eat things with "faces." They have always ground grain, but it was only when they were driven from the coast into the Outback that eating flesh became necessary.

I described a restaurant and how foods are served on decorated plates. I mentioned gravy. The idea was confusing. Why cover meat with a sauce? So I agreed to demonstrate. Of course there wasn't an appropriate pan available. Our cooking had consisted of bite-sized pieces of meat, usually placed on the sand after the coals were moved to one side. Sometimes the meat was put on skewers supported by poles. Occasionally a type of stew was constructed using meat, vegetables, herbs, and precious water. Looking around, I found a smooth, hairless sleeping skin, and with the help of Sewing Woman, we were able to create curved edges. She always carried a special pouch around her neck; it held bone needles and sinew. I melted animal fat in the center, and when it was liquid I added some fine powder they had ground earlier. I added salt grass, a crushed hot pepper seed, and finally water. It thickened, so I put it over the bite-sized meat we had served earlier, which was a very odd creature called a frilled lizard. The gravy evoked new facial expressions and comments from all who tried it. They spoke very tactfully, and at that moment my mind reverted back about fifteen years.

I had entered the Mrs. America pageant and found out that a part of the national contest was creating an original casserole recipe. For two weeks I made casseroles every day. Fourteen consecutive dinners in our home consisted of eating and evaluating the taste, appearance, and texture of each day's entry, looking for a potential award winner. My children never refused to eat, but they soon became masters of telling me tactfully what they thought. They endured some unconventional tastes in support of Mother doing her thing! When I won "Mrs. Kansas," they both shouted in celebration, "We beat the Casserole Challenge!"

Now I was seeing those same expressions on my desert companions' faces. We had fun doing almost everything we were involved in, and this was a source of great laughter as well. But because their spiritual quest is so present in everything they do, I was not surprised when someone commented how symbolic gravy was to the Mutant value system. Instead of living the truth, Mutants allow circumstances and conditions to bury universal law under a mixture of convenience, materialism, and insecurity.

The interesting thing about their remarks and observations was that I never felt I was being criticized or judged. They never judged my people as being wrong or this tribe as right. It was more like a loving adult observing a child struggling to fit a left shoe on the right foot. Who is to say you can't get a lot of mileage out of walking with shoes on incorrectly? Maybe there is valuable learning in bunions and blisters! But it does seem unnecessary suffering to an older, wiser being.

We also talked about birthday cakes and the tasty frosting. I found their analogy of icing extremely powerful. It seemed to symbolize how much time, in the one-hundred-year Mutant life span, is spent in artificial, superficial, temporary, decorative, sweetened pursuits. So very few actual moments of one's life are spent discovering who we are, and our eternal beingness.

When I spoke of birthday parties, they listened intently. I talked of the cake, songs, and gifts—an increase in candles each year as we get older. "Why would you do that?" they inquired. "To us celebration means something special. There isn't anything special about getting older. It takes no effort. It just happens!"

"If you don't celebrate getting older," I said, "what do you celebrate?"

"Getting better," was the reply. "We celebrate if we are a better, wiser person this year than last. Only you would know, so it is you who tells the others when it is time to have the party." Now that, I thought, is something I must remember!

It was truly amazing how much nutritious wild food is available and how it appears when they need it. In dried regions that appear inhospitable to vegetation, the appearance is deceptive. In the barren soil are seeds with very dense coatings. When the rains come, the seeds take root, and the landscape is transformed. Yet, within only days the flowers have completed the cycle of existence, the winds scatter the seeds, and the land returns to a harsh, parched condition.

Scattered through the desert, on the land nearer the coast and in the northern, more tropical areas, we had hearty meals using some type of bean. We found fruit and wonderful honey for our wild sassafras bark tea. At one point we peeled paper bark off trees. We used it to shelter us, to wrap around food, and to chew for its aromatic qualities that clear head colds, headaches, and mucous congestion.

Many of the bushes contained leaves with medicinal oils for treating bacterial invasions. They acted as astringents that rid the body of intestinal infections and parasites. Latex, the fluid in some plant stems and certain leaves, will remove warts, corns, and calluses. They even have alkaloids available, such as quinine. Aromatic plants are squeezed and soaked in water until the fluid changes color. It is then rubbed into the chest and back. If heated, the vapor is inhaled. They seemed to be blood cleansers, stimulants to the lymph glands, and an aid to the immune system. There is a small willowlike tree that has many aspirin characteristics. It is given for internal discomfort, for the pain accompanying a sprain or break, as well as for relief of minor muscle and joint aches and pains. It is also effective on skin lesions. There are other barks used for loose bowels, and the gum from some are dissolved in water to make cough syrup.

Overall, this particular native tribe is extremely healthy. Later, I was able to identify some of the flower petals they ate as being active against the bacteria of typhoid fever. It made me wonder if perhaps their immune systems were boosted in this way, much as our vaccines are designed to do. I do know that the Australian puff-ball, a large plant fungus, contains an anticancer substance called calvacin that is currently under research. They also have an antitumor substance called acronycine in one of the barks.

They discovered the strange properties of the wild kangaroo apple centuries ago. Modern medicine uses it as a source of the steroid solasodine in oral contraceptives. The Elder advised me that they feel very certain that new lives brought into the world are meant to be welcomed, loved, and planned. New life for the Real People tribe since the beginning of time has always been a consciously creative act. The birth of a baby means they have provided an earthly body for a fellow soul. The bodies, unlike those in our society, are not always expected to appear without flaws. It is the invisible jewel, housed within, that is flawless and both gives and receives help in the joint soul projects of becoming polished and advanced.

I felt that if they were to pray, in our understanding of petition prayer, it would be for the unloved child, not the aborted one. All souls who choose to experience human existence will be so honored, if not through one parent and that set of circumstances, then another, in another time. The Elder confided to me that the random sexual behavior among some tribes, without regard for the resulting birth, was perhaps the most backward step humankind had taken. They believe the spirit enters the fetus when it tells the world of its presence by movement. For them a stillborn child is a body that housed no spirit.

The Real People have also located a wild tobacco plant. They use the leaves for smoking in pipes on special occasions. They still use tobacco as a rare and unique substance because it is not abundant, can produce a feeling of euphoria, and can become addictive. It is symbolically used when greeting visitors or starting meetings. I saw a similarity between their respect for the tobacco weed and the Native American traditions. My friends spoke often of the earth we walked upon, reminding me it was the dust of our ancestors. They said things do not really die, things just change. They talked of how the human body returns to the ground to feed the plants, which in turn are humans' only source of breath. They seemed much more aware of the precious molecule of oxygen needed for all life than the vast majority of my American acquaintances.

The tribe of Real People have incredible eyesight. The pigment rutin, found in several of their plants, is an acceptable chemical used in ophthalmology drugs for treating fragile capillaries and blood vessels of the eye. Over the thousands of years that they had Australia to themselves, it seems they learned how food affected the body.

One problem with eating food grown in the wild is the large number of poisonous items. They recognize immediately what is off-limits. They have learned how to remove poisonous parts, but they did tell me how sad it was that some of their splintered tribes in the Aboriginal race, who have reverted to aggressive behavior, have a history of using the poison against human enemies.

When I had traveled with the group long enough, they accepted my inquiries as being sincerely necessary for my own personal understanding. I approached the subject of cannibalism. I had read the accounts in history and heard jokes from my Australian friends referring to Aborigines eating people, and even eating their own babies. Was that true, I asked?

Yes. Since the beginning of time, humans have experimented with everything. Even here on this continent, it was not possible to keep people from it. There had been Aboriginal tribes with kings, with female rulers, some who stole people away from another group, and some who ate human flesh. Mutants kill and walk away, leaving the body for disposal. The cannibals killed and used the carcass to nourish life. One group's purpose is neither better nor worse than the other. Killing a human, regardless if it's for protection, revenge, convenience, or food, is all the same. Not to kill another is what differentiates Real People from mutated human creatures.

"There is no morality in war," they said. "But cannibals never killed more in one day than they could eat. In your wars, thousands are killed in a few minutes. Perhaps it might be worth suggesting to your leaders that both parties in your war agree to five minutes of combat. Then let all the parents come to the battlefield and collect the pieces and parts of their children, take them home and mourn and bury them. After that is over, another five minutes of battle might or might not be agreed upon. It is difficult to make sense out of senselessness."

That night, as I lay on the thin means of separating my mouth and eyes from the terrain of grit, I thought about how far humankind has come in so many ways, and how far away we have drifted in so many other aspects.

12

BURIED ALIVE

COMMUNICATION WAS not a simple task. Pronouncing the tribal words was difficult. In most instances they were very long. For instance, they spoke of a tribe called Pitjantjatjara and one called Yankuntjatjara. Many things sounded identical until I learned to listen extremely carefully. I realize that reporters around the world do not agree on how to spell Aboriginal words. Some use *B, DJ, D,* and *G,* where others for the same words use *P, T, TJ,* and *K.* The point is that there is no right or wrong to it, because the people themselves do not use an alphabet. It is a no-win situation for the folks who wish to argue. My problem was that the people with whom I was walking used nasal sounds I found extremely difficult to make. To sound "ny," I learned to force my tongue against my back teeth. You will see what I mean if you do this and say the word "Indian." There is also a sound made by elevating the tongue and flicking it forward rapidly. When they sing, the sounds are often very soft and musical, but then there is a very abrupt forceful noise.

Instead of using one word for sand, they have over twenty different words, which describe textures, types, and descriptions of soil in the Outback. But a few words were easy, like *Kupi* for water. They seemed to enjoy learning my words, and they were more adept at learning my sounds than I was at learning theirs. Because they were the hosts and hostesses, I used whatever made them most comfortable. I had read in the history books Geoff had provided that when the British Colony was first established in Australia, there were two hundred different Aboriginal languages and six hundred dialects. The books didn't mention talking mind-to-mind or using hands. I used a crude form of sign language. It was the most common method of talking during the day because obviously they were sharing mind messages and telling stories by mental telepathy, so it was simply more polite to indicate something to a person walking next to me with a sign rather than disrupt with a spoken sentence. We used the universal sign of moving the fingers to say "come here," or holding up the palm for "stop," and fingers over the lips for "silence." In the first weeks together I was told to be quiet often, but eventually I learned not to ask so much and to wait to be included in the knowledge.

One day I caused a ripple of laughter through the group as we walked along. I scratched myself in response to an insect bite. They roared with comical expressions and imitated my gesture. It seemed the specific sign I used meant I had spotted a crocodile. We were at least two hundred miles from the nearest marsh.

We had been together for several weeks when I

became aware of eyes surrounding me anytime I ventured away from the group. The darker the night, the larger the eyes seemed to become. Finally the forms became clear enough for me to identify. There was a pack of vicious wild dingos on our trail.

I went running back to the camp, truly frightened for the first time, and reported my finding to Ooota. He in turn told the Elder. All the people standing nearby turned and joined our circle of concern. I waited for words, because I had learned by then that words from the Real People tribe do not automatically pour forth; they always think before they speak. I could have counted slowly to ten before Ooota relayed the message. The problem was one of odor. I had become offensive. It was true. I could smell myself and see the expression from the others. Unfortunately, I had no solution. Water was so scarce we would not waste it on bathing, nor was there a tub available. My black companions did not have the foul smell I had. I suffered with the problem, and they suffered because of me. I think part of the problem was my constantly scorching and peeling flesh and the energy being used by the burning of stored toxic fat. I was obviously losing weight daily. Of course, having no deodorant or toilet paper didn't help, and there was something else I observed. I noticed that soon after we ate, they went into the desert and emptied their bowels, and it truly did not have the strong smell that is associated with waste matter in our lifestyle. I was sure that after fifty years of my civilized diet it would take some time to detoxify my body, but I felt if I stayed in the Outback, it was possible.

I shall not forget how the Elder explained the situation to me, and the final solution. They were not concerned for themselves; they had accepted me for better or worse. Their concern was not for our safety; it was for the poor animals. I was confusing them. Ooota said the dingos believed the tribe was dragging some rotten piece of meat, and it was driving them crazy. I had to laugh because that really was the smell, like an old hunk of hamburger you left sitting in the sun.

I said I would appreciate any help they could offer. So the following day at the peak of the heat, we jointly dug a forty-five-degree angle trench, and I lay down in it. Then they covered me up completely with soil; only my face was exposed. Shade was provided, and I was left there for about two hours. Being buried, completely helpless, unable to move a muscle, is quite a feeling. It was another new experience for me. If they had walked away, I would have become a skeleton in that very spot. At first I was concerned that some curious lizard, snake, or desert rat would run up my face. For the first time in my life I truly related to a victim of paralysis, thinking about moving an arm or leg, telling an arm or leg to move, and it did not respond. But once I relaxed and closed my eyes, concentrating on releasing toxins from my body and absorbing the wonderful, cool, refreshing, cleansing elements from the ground, the time went faster.

Now I appreciate the old saying, "Necessity is the mother of invention."

It worked! We left the odor behind us in the ground.

13

HEALING

THE RAINY season was approaching. This day we spotted a cloud that stayed in view for a short period of time. It was a rare and appreciated sight. Occasionally we could even walk under the big overhead shadow, catching the same view an ant might see from the sole of a boot. It was such a delight to be among adults who had not lost the important sense of childhood fun. They would run ahead of the shadow, out into the bright sun, and taunt the cloud by teasing how slow the legs of wind were walking. Then they would come back to walk in the shade once again and tell me what a wonderful gift of cool air Divine Oneness provided for people. It was a very lighthearted and playful day. Toward the late afternoon, however, tragedy struck, or at least what appeared to me at the moment to be tragedy.

There was a young man in his midthirties called Great Stone Hunter. His talent was finding precious gems. He had recently added the "Great" because over the years he had developed the special skill of finding marvelous big opals and even gold nuggets in the mining areas after the commercial companies had abandoned the property. Real People originally felt precious metal superfluous. You could not eat it, and in a nation without markets you could not buy anything to eat with it. It was valued only for the beauty and service it might provide. However, with time, the natives found it was prized by the white man. That was even more astonishing than his strange belief that you could own and sell land. Precious gems are what provide the financing for the tribe's scout, who periodically goes into the city and brings back a report. Great Stone Hunter never ventures near any commercial operations still in business because of the haunting history of his people forced to work in the mine. They would enter on a Monday and not emerge until the end of the week. Four out of five died. They were usually charged with some crime, so were forced to work as part of a criminal sentence. There were also quotas to meet, and many times a wife and children were summoned to work with the prisoner; three people could perhaps fill the quota set for one individual. It seemed very easy to find some infraction to extend every sentence. There was no escape. It was, of course, very legal, this degradation of human lives and human flesh.

On this particular day, Great Stone Hunter was walking on the edge of an embankment when the ground gave way, and he fell off the cliff onto a rocky surface about twenty feet below. The terrain we had been walking over was made up of large sheets of naturally polished granite, layers of slab rock, and fields of gravel-sized stones.

I had, by this time, started developing a good-sized callus across the bottoms of my feet, similar to my companions' hoof appearance, but even this layer of dead tissue was not enough to make walking comfortable over jagged stones. My mind was on my feet. I was remembering a closet full of shoes back home, including hiking boots and running shoes. I heard Great Stone Hunter's cry as he tumbled through the air. We all rushed to the edge and looked down. He lay in a heap; already a dark pool of blood was visible. Several of the people rushed down into the gorge and, using a relay system, had him back on the top almost instantly. I doubt it could have worked faster if he had floated up. All their hands under him looked like a caterpillar on an assembly line.

When he was laid upon the polished slab at the top, his wound was openly displayed. It was a very severe compound fracture between the knee and ankle. The bone was protruding like a huge ugly tusk, about two inches, through the milk chocolate–colored skin. A headband came off immediately and went around the upper leg. Medicine Man and Female Healer stood on either side of the wounded patient. Other tribal members started making camp for the evening.

I inched closer and closer until I was standing next to the prostrate figure. "May I watch?" I asked. Medicine Man was moving his hands up and down the wounded leg about one inch away from the surface in a gentle gliding motion: first parallel, and then one moving from top to bottom while the other hand moved from the bottom to the top. Female Healer smiled at me and spoke to Ooota. He in turn relayed her message to me.

He explained, "This is for you. We have been told

your talent is that of female healer to your people."

"Well, I guess so," I answered. I had never been comfortable with the idea that healing comes from physicians or their bag of tricks, because I had learned years before, when I had my own health challenge with polio, that healing has only one source. Doctors can aid the body by removing foreign particles, injecting chemicals, setting and realigning bones, but that does not mean the body will heal. In fact, I am certain, there has never been a doctor anywhere, at any time, in any country, at any period in history who ever healed anything. Each person's healer is within. Doctors are at best those who have recognized an individual talent, developed it, and are privileged enough to be able to serve the community by doing what they do best and love doing. Now was not the time for a lengthy discussion however. I would accept the wording Ooota had chosen to use and agree with the natives that in my society, I, too, was regarded as a female healer.

I was told that the movement of the hands up and down, over the area of involvement, without touching, was a way of reconnecting the former pattern of the healthy leg. It would eliminate any swelling during the healing phase. Medicine Man was jogging the memory of the bone into acknowledging the true nature of its healthy state. This removed the shock created when it snapped in half, ripping away from the position developed over thirty years. They "talked" to the bone.

Next, the three main characters in this drama—Medicine Man at the foot, Female Healer kneeling at the side, and the patient on his back, resting on the earth's surface—all began to speak in prayerlike fashion. Medicine Man put both hands around the ankle. He did not appear actually to touch or pull the foot. Female Healer acted in the same capacity around the knee. Their speech was in the form of chants, or songs, each one different. At one point, in unison, they all raised their voices and shouted something. They must have used some form of traction, but I could not see any actual pulling taking place. The bone just slipped back into the hole from which it had exited. Medicine Man held the ragged skin together and motioned to Female Healer, who now began to untie the strange long tube she always carried.

Weeks before, I asked Female Healer how the women handled their monthly menses and was shown pads made from reeds, straw, and fine bird feathers. After that, from time to time, I would observe a woman leaving the group and going off alone into the desert to take care of this necessity. They buried the soiled piece just as we did our own excrement daily, in cat fashion. Occasionally, however, I had noticed a woman coming back from the desert carrying something in her palm which was taken to Female Healer. She, in turn, opened the top of the long tube she carried. I observed that it was lined with the plant leaves they used to heal my blistered and cut feet and daily sunburns. Female Healer inserted the mysterious item. The few times I was close at hand I had gotten a whiff of a terribly offensive odor. Finally I discovered what the secretly encased object was—large clots of blood passed by the women.

On this day, Female Healer did not open the top of the tube, but instead opened the bottom. There was no foul smell. There was no smell at all. She squeezed the tube into her hand and out came a black tar. It was very thick and shiny. She used it to cement the jagged edges of the wound together. She literally tarred them into place, smearing it all over the offending surface. There was no bandage, no binding, no splint, no crutch, and no sutures.

Soon the trauma was put aside, and we were busy eating our meal. During the evening, different people took turns putting Great Stone Hunter's head in their lap so he had a better view from his resting place. I also took my turn. I wanted to feel his brow and see if I could detect any fever. I also wanted to touch and be near this person who had apparently agreed to go through this demonstration of healing for my sake. His head in my lap, he looked up and winked at me.

The next morning, Great Stone Hunter stood up and walked with us. There was not a hint of a limp. The ritual they had performed, they told me, would reduce the osseous stress and prevent swelling. It had worked. For several days I looked closely at his leg and watched as the natural black compound dried and began falling off. Within five days it was gone; there were only thin scar lines where the bone had exited. This fellow weighed about one hundred forty-five pounds. How he could stand up without support on that completely severed bone and not have it come flying back out the hole was a marvel. I knew this tribe as a whole was very healthy, but they seemed to possess some special talent in dealing with crisis intervention as well.

These people with health-care talents had never studied biochemistry or pathology, but they possessed the credentials of truth, intent, and a commitment to wellness.

Female Healer asked me, "Do you understand how long forever is?"

"Yes," I said. "I understand."

"Are you certain?"

"Yes, I understand," I repeated.

"Then we can tell you something else. All humans are spirits only visiting this world. All spirits are forever beings. All encounters with other people are experiences, and all experiences are forever connections. Real People close the circle of each experience. We do not leave ends frayed as Mutants do. If you walk away with bad feelings in your heart for another person and that circle is not closed, it will be repeated later in your life. You will not suffer once but over and over until you learn. It is good to observe, to learn, and become wiser from what has happened. It is good to give thanks, as you say, to bless it, and walk away in peace."

I don't know if this man's leg bone was healed rapidly or not. There was no X ray available for pre- and post-views, and he is just a man, not a superman, but to me it didn't matter. He had no pain. He had no aftereffects, and as far as he and others were concerned, the experience was over, and we all walked away in peace and hopefully a bit wiser. The circle was closed. It was given no more energy, time, or attention.

Ooota told me they did not cause the accident. They only asked that if it was in the highest good for all life everywhere they were open to an experience where I could learn about healing by witnessing it. They didn't know if a challenge would appear or to which individual it might come, but they were open to allow me the opportunity for the experience. When it did, they were grateful once again for the gift they were allowed to share with the Mutant outsider.

I, too, was grateful that night for being allowed into

the mysterious virgin minds of these so-called uncivilized humans. I wanted to learn more about their healing techniques, but I didn't want the responsibility of adding challenges to their lives. It was clear to me that surviving in this Outback was challenge enough.

I should have known they were reading my mind and knew before I spoke what I was requesting. That night we discussed in length the connection between the physical body, the eternal part of our beingness, and a new aspect we had not touched on before, the role of feelings and emotions in health and well-being.

They believe how you feel emotionally about things is what really registers. It is recorded in every cell of the body, in the core of your personality, in your mind, and in your eternal self. Where some religions talk about the necessity of feeding the hungry and giving water to the thirsty, this tribe of people say the food and liquid being given, and the person to whom it goes, are not essential. It is the feeling you experience when you openly and lovingly give that either does or does not register. Giving water to a dying plant or animal, or giving encouragement, gains as much enlightenment for knowing life and our Creator as finding a thirsty person and providing nourishment. You leave this plane of existence with a scorecard, so to speak, that registers moment by moment how you mastered emotion. It is the invisible nonphysical feelings filling the eternal part of us that make the difference between the good and the lesser. Action is only the channel whereby the feeling, the intent, is allowed to be expressed and experienced.

In setting the bone earlier that day, the two native physicians worked by sending the thoughts of perfection to the body. There was as much going on in their heads and hearts as in their hands. The patient was open and receptive to receive wellness and believed in a state of full and immediate recovery. It was amazing to me that what appeared to be miraculous from my point of view was obviously the norm in tribal perspective. I began to wonder how much of the suffering in the United States, in illness, in the role of victims, is due to emotional programing, not, of course, on a consciously acknowledging level, but on some level of which we are unaware.

What would happen in the United States if physicians put as much faith in the healing ability of the human body as they do in believing drugs can or cannot cure? More and more I appreciated the importance of the doctor/patient bond. If the physician doesn't believe the person can get well, that belief alone may cripple the task. I learned long ago that when a doctor tells a patient there is no cure, that really means, in the doctor's education and background, there is no information available to use for a cure. It doesn't mean there is no cure. If any other person has ever overcome the same disorder, then the human body obviously has the capability to heal. In a long discussion with Medicine Man and Female Healer I discovered an incredible new perspective on health or illness. "Healing has absolutely nothing to do with time," I was told. "Both healing and disease take place in an instant." My interpretation of what they were saying was that your body is whole, well, and healthy on a cellular level, and then in an instant, the first derangement or abnormality happens in a part of some one cell. It may take months or years for the symptoms or diagnosis to be recognized. And healing is the reverse process. You are ill and your health is declining and then, depending upon what society you are in, you receive some sort of treatment. In an instant the body stops going downhill and begins the first step of repair. The Real People tribe believes that we are not random victims of ill health, that the physical body is the only means our higher level of eternal consciousness has to communicate with our personality consciousness. Slowing down the body allows us to look around and analyze the really important wounds we need to mend: wounded relationships, gaping holes in our belief system, walled-up tumors of fear, eroding faith in our Creator, hardened emotions of unforgiveness, and so on.

I thought of the American doctors who are doing work now with positive mental imaging in treating cancer patients. Most of them are not very popular within their peer groups. What they are exploring is too "new." Here was an example of the oldest people on earth using techniques that had been handed down through eons of time and proving their value. Yet, we so-called civilized folks don't want to use positive thought transference because it might be just a fad, and we cautiously agree it would be better to wait awhile and see how it works out on a few select conditions. When a critically ill Mutant has been given all the doctor's available treatments and is on the brink of death, the physician tells the family that everything within his or her power has been done. It is true, how many times I have heard the remark, "I'm sorry, there's nothing more we can do. Now it is in the hands of God." Funny how backward that seems to be.

I don't believe the Real People are superhuman in their approach and treatment of illness and accidents. I sincerely believe everything they do can be explained in our scientific analysis. It is just that we are striving to create machines to accomplish certain techniques, and the Real People are proof it can be done without an electrical cord.

Humankind is wandering around, struggling, but on the continent of Australia the most sophisticated health-care techniques are happening only a few thousand miles from the ancient practices that have saved lives for all time. Perhaps someday they will unite and a full circle of knowledge will emerge.

What a day for global celebration!

14

~~~~~~~~~~~~~~~~~~~~~~~~

TOTEMS

DURING THE day the wind shifted and gained in intensity, and we struggled as sand pelted against our bodies. Our tracks on the earth surface vanished the moment they appeared. I strained to see past the red dust. It was like a vision through bloodshot lenses. Finally we found shelter along the side of a rocky ridge and huddled to protect ourselves from the harsh treatment. Wrapped in skins, sitting eye-to-eye, I asked, "What exactly is your relationship to the animal kingdom? Are they your totems, your emblems that are reminders of ancestry?"

"We are all one," was the reply, "learning strength from weakness."

I was told the brown falcon that continued to follow us reminded the people that sometimes we believe in what we see immediately ahead of us. If we only lift ourselves and soar higher, we can see a view where a much bigger picture is taking place. They told me that Mutants who die in the desert because they see no water, and become angry and despondent, actually die from emotion.

The Real People tribe believes humans still have evolutionary learning to do as a global family. They believe the universe is still unfolding and not a finished project. Humans seem too busy being to become *beings*.

They spoke of the kangaroo—the silent, usually gentle creature that grows from two to seven feet tall and is found in earth colors of soft silver-gray to copper red. At birth the red kangaroo is the size and weight of one kidney bean, yet at maturity it stands seven feet tall. They think Mutants make too much of skin colors and body shapes. The main lesson taken from the kangaroo is that it does not step backward. It is not possible for it. It always goes forward, even when going around in circles! Its long tail is like the trunk of a tree and bears its weight. Many people choose kangaroo as their totem because they feel a real kinship and recognize the necessity of learning balance in their personality. I liked the idea of looking back over my life and considering, even when it appeared I had made mistakes or poor choices; on some level of my being, it was the best I could do at the time. In the long run it was going to prove to be a step forward. The kangaroo also controls reproduction and ceases to multiply when environmental conditions warrant.

The slithering snake is a learning tool when we observe its frequent removal of the outer skin. Little is gained in a lifetime if what you believe at age seven is still how you feel at age thirty-seven. It is necessary to shed old ideas, habits, opinions, and even companions sometimes. Letting go is sometimes a very difficult human lesson. The snake is no lesser nor greater for shedding the old. It is just necessary. New things cannot come where there is no room. He looks and feels younger when he strips himself of old baggage. He isn't younger, of course. The Real People laughed because keeping track of age seems senseless to this tribe. The snake is a master of charm and power. Both are good to have but can be destructive when they become overwhelming. There are many poisonous snakes whose poison can be used to kill people. It works well for that, but like so many things it can also be used for a meaningful purpose, such as helping the person who has fallen into an ant mound, or someone tortured by wasps or bees. Real People respect the snake's need for privacy in the same way each of them requires some time alone.

The emu is a big, powerful, flightless bird. It helps the harvest of food because it is a fruit eater; by voiding seeds as it travels, we enjoy widespread abundance of plant foods. It also lays a large green-black egg; it is a totem of fertility.

The dolphin is very dear to the Real People tribe, although they no longer have much access to the sea. The dolphin was the first creature with whom they could experience talking head-to-head, and it shows that life is meant to be happy and free. They learned from this master of games that there is no competition, no loser, no winners, only fun for all.

The spider's lesson is never to be greedy. It shows that objects of necessity can be objects of beauty and art as well. The spider also teaches that we can become too easily enraptured with ourselves.

We talked about the lessons of the ant, the rabbit, the lizards, even the wild brumbie—the wild horse of Australia. When I spoke of certain animals becoming extinct, they asked if Mutants did not realize that the end of each species is a step closer to the end of the human species.

Finally, the sandstorm ended. We dug ourselves out. Then they told me that agreement had been made about my animal kinship. It was determined from watching my shadow, my manner, and the stride I had acquired upon my developing padded feet. They said they would draw the animal for me in the sand. While the sun shone like a spotlight before me, they used their fingers and toes as pencils. The outline of a head appeared, someone added little round ears. They looked at my nose and projected that shape onto the sand. Spirit Woman drew the eyes and told me they were the color of mine. Then spotted markings were added, and I teased, saying my freckles were all covered up now. "We do not know what this animal is," they said. "It does not exist in Australia." They felt the female of the perhaps mythical species would be the hunter, and she would travel alone comfortably much of the time. She would put the welfare of her cubs before her own life, or that of her mate. Then, smiling, Ooota added, "When this animal's necessities are met, it is gentle, but its sharp teeth do not go unused."

I looked down at the finished picture and saw a cheetah. "Yes," I said. "I know this animal." I could relate to all the teachings from that big cat.

I remember how still it seemed that night; and I reasoned the brown falcon, too, must be at rest.

A crescent moon was hanging in the cloudless sky when I discovered our day had passed as we were talking instead of walking.

15

BIRDS

SISTER TO Bird Dreaming stepped into the morning circle. She was offering to share her talent with the group if that was in the best interest of all concerned. If it was, Divine Oneness would provide. We had not seen a bird for two or three weeks except for my faithful friend, the brown falcon with the dark velvet wings, who came swooping over our moving group and always came nearest my head.

The people were very excited about the event, and by then I, too, believed birds would appear out of nowhere if that was in the plan for our day.

The sun had cast its bright orange halfway down the side of the distant hills when we saw them approaching. It was a flock of very colorful birds, bigger than the parakeets I used to keep in a cage at home, and similar in the variety of colors. They were so numerous it was impossible to see blue sky between the flapping wings. Suddenly the sound of boomerangs hissing in the sky was combined

with the language from the fowls. It sounded like the
birds were clamoring insistently, "Me, me, me." They fell
from the sky in groups of twos and threes. Not one single
bird lay on the ground suffering. They were killed
instantly.

That night we had a wonderful meal, and the group
was provided with multicolored feathers. They made
headbands and chest plates, and used some to construct
pads for women for use during their monthly menses. We
ate the meat. The brains were scooped out and kept separate. They were dried and used later, some mixed in the
herbal medicines, and some mixed with water and oil in
the tanning processes. The few leftover parts were put out
for the group of wild dingo dogs that trailed us from time
to time.

There was no waste. Everything was recycled back
into nature and back into the earth. This was one picnic
that left no trash; in fact, you could barely tell we had
ever camped and eaten at any of our sites.

They are masters of blending in, using yet leaving the
universe undisturbed.

16

~~~~~~~~~~~~~~~~~~~

SEWING

WE HAD finished our meal for the day. The fire was a soft glow of embers, and occasional sparks rose into the surrounding limitless sky. Several of us sat in a circle around the flickering patterns. These people, like many Native American tribes, believe when you are sitting in a circle it is very important that you observe the other members of the group, most especially the person sitting directly opposite you. That person is a spirit reflection of yourself. The things you see in that individual that you admire are qualities within yourself that you wish to make more dominant. The actions, appearances, and behavior that you do not like are things about yourself that need working on. You cannot recognize what you deem to be good or bad in others unless you yourself have the same strengths and weaknesses at some level of your being. Only the degree of self-discipline and self-expression differ. They believe the only way a person ever truly changes anything about himself is by his own decision, and that everyone has the ability to change anything he wants to about his personality. There is no limit to what you can release and what you can acquire. They also believe the only true influence you have on anyone else is by your own life, how you act, what you do. Believing this way makes the tribal members committed every day to being better persons.

I was sitting across from Sewing Master. Her head bent as she gave serious concentration to the repair job at hand. Earlier in the day, Great Stone Hunter had come to her after the water vessel he carried around his waist belt suddenly fell to the ground. It was not the kangaroo bladder filled with our precious cargo that wore out, only the leather strap holding it to his side.

Sewing Master cut the natural thread with her teeth. They were worn smooth and about half their original height. Raising her head from the working posture, she said, "It is interesting, Mutants and aging. Jobs one grows too old to perform. Limited usefulness."

"Never too old for worth," someone added.

"It seems business has become a hazard to Mutants. Your businesses were started so people could get better items collectively than they could get for themselves and as a method to express individual talent, and become part of your money system. But now the goal of business is to stay in business. It seems so strange to us because we see the product as a real thing, and people as real things, but business isn't real. A business is only an idea, only an agreement, yet the goal of business is to stay in business regardless. Such beliefs are difficult to understand," Sewing Master commented.

So I told them about the free-enterprise system of government, private ownership, corporations, stocks and bonds, unemployment benefits, social security, and unions. I told them what I knew about the Russian form of government, and how the Chinese and Japanese economies differ. I have lectured in Denmark, Brazil, Europe, and Sri Lanka, so I shared what I knew about life in those places.

We talked about industry and products. They all agreed, automobiles were handy objects of transportation. Being a slave to the payment of it, however, and possibly being involved in an accident where you would most certainly have a confrontation to settle, possibly creating an enemy, and sharing the limited desert water with four wheels and a seat, wasn't worth it, in their opinion. Besides they are never in a hurry.

I looked at Sewing Master sitting across from me. She had many remarkable traits I admired. She was well versed on the history of the world and even on current events, yet she did not read or write. She was creative. I noticed she offered to make the necessary repair for Great Stone Hunter before he asked. She was a woman with a purpose; she lived that purpose. It seemed true; I could learn from observing the one sitting opposite me in the circle.

I wondered what she thought of me. When we formed a circle, someone always sat opposite me but there was never a big rush for the position. One major flaw, I knew, was asking too many questions. I needed to remember that these people shared openly, so when the time was right, I would be included. I probably sounded like some pesty child.

After we had retired for the night, I was still thinking about her remarks. Business is not real, it is just an agreement, yet the goal of business is to stay in business regardless of the outcome on the people or the product and services! That was quite an astute observation for someone who has never read a newspaper, seen a television, or listened to the radio. At that moment I wished the entire world could hear this woman.

Maybe instead of calling this place the Outback, they should consider it the center of human concern.

17

~~~~~~~~~~~~~~~~~~~

MEDICINE OF MUSIC

SEVERAL PEOPLE in the group possessed the medicine of music. Medicine was the word used in the translation sometimes. It didn't mean medicinal, nor was it related only to physical healing. Medicine was anything good that one contributed to the overall welfare of the group. Ooota explained it was good to have the talent, or medicine, for setting broken bones, but that was no better, or lesser, than the talent of having kinship to fertility and eggs. Both were needed, and both were uniquely personal. I agreed and looked forward to a future meal of eggs.

That day I was advised that a great musical concert was to take place. We carried no instruments in our meager possessions, but I had long ago ceased to question how and where things would appear.

That afternoon I could feel the excitement build as we walked through a canyon. It was narrow, perhaps twelve feet wide with walls extending up eighteen feet. We stopped for the night, and while the vegetable and insect meal was being prepared the musicians set up their stage. Round barrel-shaped plants grew there. Someone cut off the tops and scooped out the moist pumpkin-colored centers, which we all sucked. The large seeds in the pulp were put to one side. Some of the hairless skins we carried were draped over the plants, tied securely. They became incredible percussion instruments.

An old dead tree lay nearby, several of the limbs covered with termites. One was broken off and the insects knocked off. The termites had eaten the center out of the branch, and it was filled with sawdust. By using a stick in a ramming motion and then blowing out the dead crumbly core, they soon had a long hollow tube. I felt I was seeing Gabriel's trumpet constructed. I found out later that this is what the Australians commonly refer to as a didjeridoo. It makes a low musical sound when you blow into it.

One of the musicians started clicking sticks together, and another used two rocks to establish a beat. They had taken pieces of shale, hung them from threads, and created the sound of tinkling chimes. One man made a bull-roarer, which is a flat piece of wood attached to a cord; it is whirled around, making a roaring noise. They expertly controlled the increasing and decreasing of the volume. The arrangement in the canyon created a fantastic vibration and echo. The word *concert* could not have been more aptly used.

The people sing individually, in groups, and often in harmony. I realized some of the songs were as old as time. These people repeat chants created here in the desert before the invention of our calendar. But I also experienced new compositions, music being composed just because I was there. I was told, "Just as a musician seeks musical expression, so the music in the universe seeks to be expressed."

Because they have no written language, knowledge is passed from generation to generation in song and dance. Each historical event can be depicted by drawings on the sand or in music and drama. They have music every day because it is necessary to keep facts fresh in the memory, and to tell their entire history takes about a year. If each event were also painted and all the paintings were laid on the ground in the proper sequence, you would have a map of the world as it has appeared over the last thousands of years.

What I really witnessed, however, was how these people live life to the fullest without any material attachments. At the end of our festival, the instruments were replaced where they had found them. The seeds were planted to insure new growth. Signs were painted on the rock wall, indicating the harvest available for the next travelers. The sticks, limb, and rocks were released by the musicians, yet the joy of creative composition, and the talent, remained as a confirmation of each person's worth and self-esteem. A musician carries the music within him. He needs no specific instrument. He is the music.

It seemed to me that day I was also learning that life is self-service. We can enrich our own lives, give to ourselves, and be as creative and happy as we will allow ourselves to be. Composer and the other musicians walked away with heads held high. "Pretty great concert," one musician commented. "One of the finest," was the reply. I heard the featured individual say, "Guess before too long,

I'll change my name from Composer to Great Composer."

It wasn't an inflated ego I was observing. These are merely people who recognize their talents and the importance of sharing and developing the numerous wonders we are given. There is an important connection between acknowledging one's own self-worth and the celebration of personally bestowing a new name.

These people say they have been here for all time. Scientists know they have inhabited Australia for at least fifty thousand years. It is truly amazing that after fifty thousand years they have destroyed no forests, polluted no water, endangered no species, caused no contamination, and all the while they have received abundant food and shelter. They have laughed a lot and cried very little. They live long, productive, healthy lives and leave spiritually confident.

18

~~~~~~~~~~~~~~

DREAM CATCHER

ONE MORNING started with an air of excitement as the small group formed our routine pattern, facing east. Only a hint of color indicated impending dawn. Spirit Woman walked to the center and replaced the Tribal Elder who had concluded his portion of morning worship.

Spirit Woman and I had a lot in common physically. She was the only Aboriginal female in the entire tribe weighing over 120 pounds. I was sure I was losing weight, walking in the intense heat and eating only one meal per day. I had enough excess adipose tissue stored throughout my body that I quite liked the picture of fat dripping off and surrounding my footprints in the sand.

In the center of our semicircle Spirit Woman stood, hands extended over her head, offering her talent to the invisible audience in the sky. She opened herself to be a means of expression if Divine Oneness were to operate through her that day. She desired to share her talent with me, the adopted Mutant on this walkabout. The petition concluded, she loudly and emphatically gave thanks. The others in the group joined, shouting gratitude for the yet unmanifested gifts of the day. Normally, I was told, this would be done in silence, using their perfected head-talk, but because I was still a novice at receiving mental telepathy, and a guest, they performed within the framework of my limitations.

We walked that day until late afternoon. There had been very little vegetation growing along our route. It was a relief for me, however, not to have spinifex blades injecting their barbs into the soles of my feet.

Silence was broken in late afternoon when someone spotted a grove of dwarf trees. They were strange-looking plants, a tree trunk that spread out on top like a giant bush. This was what Spirit Woman had asked for and had been anticipating.

The previous night, as we sat around the fire, she and three others had each taken a flat hide surface and stitched it solidly to a rim. Today they carried the finished objects. I did not ask the purpose. I knew I would be told in time.

Spirit Woman grabbed my hand and pulled me over to the trees, pointing. I looked, seeing nothing. Her excitement drew my attention back for a second search. Then I saw it, a giant spider web. It was a thick, glistening, complex design involving hundreds of woven strands. There seemed to be one on several of the trees. She spoke to Ooota, who in turn told me to choose one. I did not know what I should be looking for but had learned that choosing intuitively was the way of the Aborigines. I pointed to one.

Next she took an aromatic oil from the pouch she carried at her waist and smeared it all over the round tambourine-shaped object. She pulled away all the leaves behind the target of her attention. Then, placing the oiled surface behind the web, with one swift swoop forward, she emerged with the web captured perfectly and framed professionally on the hide. I watched as others came forward and selected a web, and each of the women, carrying a frame, recreated the scene of whisking the gossamer threads onto the ready-made mounting.

While we had been playing, the rest of the tribe had been busy building a fire and gathering food for our evening meal. It included many of the large spiders from the dwarf trees, some roots, and a new tuber I had not eaten before that resembled a turnip.

After our meal, we gathered around as we did each evening. Spirit Woman explained her talent to me. Every human being is unique, and each of us is given certain characteristics that are exceptionally strong and can become a talent in life. Her contribution to the society was that of Dream Catcher. Everyone dreams, I was told. Not everyone cares to remember their dreams or learn the information from them, but everyone does dream. "Dreams are the shadow of reality," she said. Everything that exists, that happens here, is also available in the dream world. All answers are there. These special webs are helpful in a ceremony of song and dance to aid in asking the universe for dream guidance. Spirit Woman then assists the dreamer to understand the message.

I understood them to say that the word *dreaming* means levels of awareness. There is ancestor dreaming when thought created the world; there is out-of-body dreaming such as deep meditation, there is sleep dreaming, and so on.

The tribe uses the dream catchers to ask for guidance in any situation. If they want help in understanding a relationship, a health question, or the purpose behind some experience, they believe the answer can be brought to light in a dream. Mutants know only one way to enter the dream state and that is sleep, but the Real People are aware of dream consciousness while awake. Without the use of mind-controlling drugs, merely using breath techniques and concentration, they perform consciously while in the dream world.

The instructions I received were to dance with the dream catcher. Whirling is especially successful. You plant the question firmly in your mind and ask it over and over as you move about. The most effective spin, and the Aboriginal explanation for it, is an exercise that increases energy vortexes in seven key centers of the body: merely standing with my arms outstretched and spinning always to the right.

Soon dizzy, I sat down and reflected how my life had changed. Out here where there was not even one person per square kilometer, in an area more than three times the size of Texas, I was performing a whirling dervish, kicking up the sand and causing the air that contacted my dream catcher to ripple endlessly across the open expanse.

The tribal people do not dream at night unless they call in a dream. Sleep for them is a time for important rest and recovery of the body. It is not meant to be a time of splitting energy between projects. They believe the reason Mutants dream at night is because in our society we are not allowed to dream during the day, and especially to dream with one's eyes open is totally misunderstood.

Finally it was time to sleep. I smoothed out the sand and used my arm as a pillow. I was handed a small container of water and told to drink one-half of it now and the remainder upon awakening. That would help me remember the dream in detail. The question that was most pressing on my mind was the question I asked. What am I to do, after this journey is concluded, with the information I am being given?

In the morning Spirit Woman, speaking through Ooota, asked me to recall my dream. I thought it would be impossible for her to help interpret the meaning because it did not contain anything that seemed related to Australia, but I told her about it anyway. She asked me mostly about how I felt, what emotion was attached to the objects and things that happened in my dream. It was remarkable how she could draw insight from me, when the civilized lifestyle I had dreamed of was totally foreign to her.

I came to the understanding that there would be some storms in my life, that people and things I had invested a lot of time and energy into were going to be laid aside, but now I knew what it felt like to be a centered, peaceful being, and I had that emotion to draw upon anytime I needed or wanted it. I learned I could live more than one life in a lifetime and that I had already experienced the closing of a door. I learned that a time had come where I could no longer stay with the people, the location, the values and beliefs I held. For my own soul growth I had gently closed a door and entered a new place, a new life that was equal to a step up a spiritual rung on a ladder. And most important, I did not have to do anything with the information. If I simply lived the principles that appeared to be truth for me, I would touch the lives of those I was destined to touch. The doors would be opened. After all "it" was not my message; I was merely the messenger.

I wondered if any of the others who had danced with the dream catcher would share their dreams. Before I could ask the question, Ooota read my mind and said, "Yes, Tool Maker wishes to speak." Tool Maker was an elderly man who specialized in making not only tools, but paintbrushes, cooking gear, and just about everything. His question had been about muscle aches. His dream had been about a turtle that crawled out of the billabong to discover he had lost legs on one side of his body and was lopsided. After Spirit Woman talked him through the dream, like she had done with me, he came to the conclusion it was time for him to teach someone else his trade. He once had loved the responsibility of being a master craftsman, but now there was less true enjoyment and more self-inflicted pressure, so he was signaled a need for change. He had become one-sided, no longer balanced in work and play.

I saw him teaching others in the days that followed, and when I asked about his aches and pains, his withered face increased in deep lines, as smiling he said, "When thinking became flexible, joints became flexible. No pain, no more."

19

━━━∿∿∿∿∿∿∿∿∿∿∿∿∿∿∿∿━━━

DINNER SURPRISE

IT WAS during our morning prayer ritual that Kindred to Large Animals spoke. His brotherhood wished to be honored. All agreed; they had not heard from them in some time.

In Australia there aren't very many large animals. It is not like Africa with elephants, lions, giraffe, and zebra. I was curious to see what the universe had in store.

That day we walked at a brisk pace. The heat seemed less concentrated, perhaps even a few degrees below one hundred. Female Healer put a thick lizard and plant oil combination on my face and nose and especially on the tops of my ears. I had not counted layers of skin but knew I had gone through several. Actually, I was concerned that eventually I would have no ears left because the sunburning never seemed to cease. Spirit Woman came to my rescue. They called for a problem-solving meeting, and although this situation was unique for them, they rapidly came up with a solution. A gadget was created that resembled old-fashioned earmuffs worn in the snow. Spirit Woman took an animal ligament, tied it in a circle, and Sewing Woman attached feathers all around it. This was hung over my ears, and combined with the oil, it provided wonderful relief.

The day was fun. We played guessing games as we traveled. They took turns imitating animals and reptiles or acting out events from the past, and we tried to solve each riddle. There was laughter all day long. Footprints of my traveling companions no longer looked like pox marks on the sand; I was beginning to see the slight variations characteristic of each person's unique carriage.

As evening approached, I began searching the distant plain for vegetation. The color ahead of us was changing from beige ground cover to shades of green. Then I saw some trees as we approached a new terrain. You would think by then I would no longer be surprised as I witnessed how things manifested out of nowhere for Real People. But their genuine enthusiasm at the receipt of each gift had become a part of my core personality.

There they stood, the large animals who wished to be honored for their purpose of existence—four wild camels. They each had a single tall hump and were not at all groomed like the ones I had seen in the circus and at the zoo. Camels are not native to Australia. They were brought here for the purpose of transportation, and apparently some of them had survived, though the party riding them did not.

The tribe stopped. Six scouts went off, divided. Three approached from the east and three from the west. They silently crept forward in a hunched position. Each carried a boomerang, a spear, and a spear thrower. The spear thrower is a separate wooden item that launches the spear. By using the full arm motion, as well as the snap from the wrist, the spear distance and capability for precise accuracy is tripled. The herd of camels had one male, two adult females, and a half-grown member.

The keen eyes of the hunters surveyed the pack. They advised me later that they had agreed mentally it was the elderly female who was to be taken. They use the ways of their brother animal, the dingo, to receive signals from the weakest animal. It seems to call to the hunters, the desire to be honored that day for its purpose of being and to leave the strong to continue the lifeline. Without words, and no hand signals that I observed, in totally coordinated timing, the rushed advance took place. A perfectly planted spear to the head and a simultaneous one to the chest brought instant death. The three remaining camels galloped away, the sound of hooves disappearing in the distance.

We prepared a deep pit, lined the bottom and sides with layers of dry grass. Kindred to Large Animals, knife in hand, sliced open the belly of the camel in zipperlike style. A pocket of warm air escaped, and with it came the strong, warm odor of blood. The organs were removed one by one, heart and liver set aside. These were valued by the tribe for the properties of strength and endurance they contained. As a scientist, I could see the tremendous source of iron they brought to a diet that was inconsistent and unpredictable in nutrients. Blood was funneled into a special container carried around the neck of Female Healer's younger apprentice. The hooves were put to one side, and I was told they were very useful, having numerous purposes. I couldn't imagine what they were.

"Mutant, this camel grew into adulthood just for you," one of the butchers shouted. He held up the enormous, watery bladder pouch.

My addiction to water was well known, and they kept looking for an appropriate bladder to make into a vessel for me to carry. One was now available.

This land was obviously a favorite grazing spot for animals, as indicated by the piles of dung. Ironically, I now treasured what only months before had been repulsive objects even for me to discuss. Today I picked up dung, grateful for this wonderful source of fuel.

Our joyful day was ending with more laughter and jokes as they debated about my carrying the camel bladder tied to my waist, around my neck, or wearing it like a backpack. The next day we marched with the camel hide stretched over the heads of several people. It provided shade but also allowed the hide to dry and cure as we continued our journey. They had stripped the hide of all visible flesh and treated it with tannin collected from plant bark. The camel had provided more meat than we needed for our meal, so the rest was cut into strips. Some of it had not cooked well in the pit, and that portion was strung on a tree-limb pole.

Several of us carried these banners across the desert—camel flesh flapping in the wind, drying out and becoming naturally preserved.

An odd parade indeed!

20

UNCHOCOLATE-COVERED ANTS

THE SUN shone in such a scorching glare I could not force my eyelids fully open. Sweat, produced in every cell of my skin, escaped to run in minirivers down the creases of my chest to moisten my thighs as they rubbed together with every step. Even the tops of my feet were perspiring. I had never seen that before; it was an indication to me we had lost the 110-degree comfort and were experiencing nearly unbearable temperatures. The bottoms of my feet had also formed a strange pattern. There were blisters from toe-to-heel and side-to-side, but blisters had formed underneath the already bubbled surface; my feet felt dead.

As we walked, a woman disappeared into the desert for a few moments and reappeared carrying an enormous bright green leaf. It was about a foot and a half wide. I saw no plant in sight from which the leaf could have come. It was fresh and healthy. Everything surrounding us was brown, brittle, and dry. No one questioned where she found it. Her name was Bearer of Happiness; her talent in life was conducting games. That evening she was to be in charge of our sharing time, and she said we were going to play the game of creation.

We came across a mound of ants, big ones, probably an inch long, with strange, distended centers. I was told, "You are going to love this taste!" These creatures were to be honored as a part of our dinner. They are a variety of honey ant, and the distended stomachs hold a sweet substance that tastes much like honey. They never become as large and sweet-tasting as the ones that inhabit ground closer to lush vegetation. Nor is the honey a thick and creamy, bright yellow goo. Instead, they seem to have extracted their substance from the colorless heat and wind of our surroundings. These ants are probably the closest thing to the sweet taste of a candy bar this clan ever experiences. The people put out their arms and let the ants crawl on them and then stick their hands in their mouths. As they are withdrawn the insects are sucked off. Their expressions told me it must taste wonderful. I knew sooner or later they would think it was time for me to try one, so I decided to be daring. I took just one and plopped it in. The trick was to crush the critter in your mouth and enjoy the sweetness, not to swallow it whole. I couldn't manage either. I couldn't get past all the legs wiggling around on my tongue and the ant crawling up onto my gums. I spit it out. Later, when we had a fire, they put ants into a leaf enclosure, buried it in the coals and, when cooked, I licked it off the surface of the container like a melted Hershey Bar off the wrapper. For anyone who hasn't eaten orange-blossom honey, it probably would be a treat. However, it wouldn't sell very well in the city!

That night Game Woman tore the leaf into pieces. She didn't count them in the traditional sense that we do, but she provided one for each person in her own method of keeping track. While she did this, we were making music and singing songs. Then the game began.

While chanting continued, the first piece was laid on the sand. Then another and another until the music stopped. We all observed the design forming like a jigsaw puzzle. As more pieces were put on the ground, it became apparent the rules included moving any portion, if you felt your piece was better suited to that spot. There were no specific turns. It really was a noncompetitive group-oriented project. Soon the top half of the leaf was completed and back to its original formation. At that point everyone congratulated everyone else, we shook hands, hugged, and whirled around. The game was half over, and everyone had participated. Concentration began again, and we were down to serious business. I walked up to the pattern and laid down my part. Later I walked to the design again but couldn't locate which piece was mine, so I returned and sat down. Ooota read my mind and, without asking, he told me, "It is okay. It only appears the pieces of leaf are separate, as people appear separate, but we are all one. That is why it is the game of creation."

He interpreted as several people advised me. "To be one does not mean we are all the same. Each being is unique. No two occupy the same space. As the leaf needs all the parts for completion, so each spirit has its special place. People can try to maneuver, but in the end each will return to the right place. Some of us seek a straight path, while others enjoy the weariness of making circles."

I became aware that the people were all looking at me, and in my mind came the idea to get up and go to the pattern. When I did, there was only one space left uncovered, and the portion of leaf needed was laying a few inches away. I put the last piece into the puzzle, and a shout of joy resounded through the uncluttered surroundings and out into the vast expanse of open space that encircled our small group of human beings.

In the distance a group of dingos raised their pointed faces upward and howled into the black velvet sky dotted with the sparkles of celestial diamonds.

"Your finish confirms your right to this walk. We journey a straight path in Oneness. Mutants have many beliefs; they say your way is different from my way, your savior is not my savior, your forever is not my forever. But the truth is, all life is one life. There is only one game in progress. There is one race, many different shades. Mutants argue the name of God, what building, what day, what ritual. Did He come to Earth? What do his stories mean? Truth is truth. If you hurt someone, you hurt self. If you help someone, you help self. Blood and bone is in all people. It's the heart and intent that is different. Mutants think about this one hundred years only, of self and separateness. Real people think about forever. It is all one, our ancestors, our unborn grandchildren, all of life everywhere."

After the game was over, one of the men asked me if it was true some people live their entire lives and never know what their God-given talents are? I had to admit I had patients who were very depressed, who felt life had passed them by, but others had made a contribution. Yes, I had to admit, many Mutants did not think they were given any talent, and they did not think about the purpose of life until they were dying. Big tears came into his eyes as he shook his head, showing how difficult it was to believe such a thing could happen.

"Why can't Mutants see, if my song makes one person happy, it is a good job? You help one person, good job. Can only help one at a time anyway."

I asked if they had ever heard the name Jesus. "Certainly," I was told. "The missionaries taught: Jesus is the Son of God. Our eldest brother. Divine Oneness in human form. He receives the greatest veneration. Oneness came to the earth many years ago to tell the Mutants how to live, what they had forgotten. Jesus did not come to the Real People tribe. He certainly could have, we were right here, but it wasn't our message. It didn't apply to us because we have not forgotten. We were already living His Truth. To us," they continued, "Oneness is not a thing. Mutants seem addicted to form. They can't accept anything invisible and without a shape. God, Jesus, Oneness for us is not an essence that surrounds things or is present inside of things—it is everything!"

Life and living according to the tribe is in movement, advancement, and change. They spoke about alive and nonalive time. People are nonliving when angry, depressed, feeling sorry for themselves, or filled with fear. Breathing doesn't determine being alive. It just tells others which body is ready for burial or not! Not all breathing people are in a state of aliveness. It's okay to try out negative emotions and see how they feel, but it certainly isn't a place one would wisely want to stay. When the soul is in human form you get to play—to see how it feels to be happy or sad, jealous or grateful, and so on. But you are supposed to learn from the experience and ultimately figure out which feels painful and which feels great.

Next we talked about games and sports. I told them that in the United States we are very interested in sporting events, that in fact we pay ballplayers much more than we pay schoolteachers. I told them I could demonstrate a game and suggested we all make a line and run as fast as we could. The one who runs the fastest will become the winner. The people looked at me intently with their beautiful big dark eyes, then they looked at each other. Finally someone said, "But if one person wins, everyone else must lose. Is that fun? Games are for fun. Why would you submit anyone to such an experience and then try to convince him he was in truth a winner? That custom is difficult to understand. Does it work for your people?" I just smiled and shook my head "no."

There was a dead tree nearby, so I asked for assistance, and we constructed a teeter-totter by placing a long limb over a tall rock. It was great fun, and even the oldest members of the group took a turn moving up and down. They pointed out to me there are some things you just can't do alone, and using this toy was one of them! Seventy-, eighty-, ninety-year-old people had released the child within and had fun playing games not designed for winners and losers, but for everyone's enjoyment.

I also taught them to jump rope using several flexible, long animal-gut ropes tied together. We tried marking off a court in the sand for learning hopscotch, but it was too dark and our bodies were demanding rest. We postponed that treat for another time.

That night I stretched out on my back and looked up at the incredible sparkling sky. Not even a display of diamonds on a jeweler's black velvet showcase could be more impressive. My attention was drawn like a magnet to the brightest one. It seemed to open my mind in realizing that these people do not grow old like we do. True, their bodies wear out eventually, but it is more like a candle burning down slowly and evenly. They don't have one organ giving out at age twenty and another at forty. What we call stress in the United States seemed a cop-out now.

My body was finally cooling off. Lots of sweat was going into this learning, but it was indeed powerful instruction. How could I share with my society what I was witnessing here? People would never believe me. I had to be ready for that. People would find this way of life hard to believe. But somehow, I knew that the importance of healing physical health must be coupled with the real healing of humans, the healing of their wounded, bleeding, diseased, and injured eternal beingness.

I stared at the sky, asking myself, "How?"

21

OUT IN FRONT

THE SUN popped up, and with it came instant thermal heat. That morning the daily rituals were special. I was placed in the center position of our semicircle facing east. Ooota told me to acknowledge Divine Oneness in my own way and send out my prayer for the goodness of the day. At the conclusion of the ceremony, while we prepared to walk, I was told it was my turn to lead. I was to walk in front and lead the tribe. "But I can't," I said. "I don't know where we are going or how to find anything. I really appreciate the offer, but I just can't lead."

"You should," I heard. "It is time. In order to know your home, the earth, all its levels of life, and your relationship to everything seen and unseen, you must lead. It is fine to walk for a while as the last one in any group, and it is acceptable to spend time mingling in the middle, but ultimately everyone must at some time lead. You have no way of understanding leadership roles until you assume that responsibility. Everyone must experience all of these roles at some time, without exception, sooner or later, if not in this lifetime, sometime! The only way to pass any test is to take the test. All tests on every level are always repeated one way or another until you pass."

So we began to walk with me assuming the lead position. It was a very hot day. The temperature seemed higher than 105 degrees. At midday we stopped and used our nightly sleeping material to make shade. After the peak of the heat was over, we walked again, long past our usual time for making camp. No plants or animals appeared along our route to be honored as our meal. We found no water. The air remained a hot, motionless vacuum. Finally I gave up and called the day's journey to a halt.

That night I asked for help. We had no food, no water. I asked Ooota, but he ignored me. I asked others, knowing they could not understand my language, but knowing they could understand what my heart was saying. I said, "Help me, Help us!" I repeated it over and over, but no one responded.

Instead they talked about how every person at some time walks in the rear. I began to wonder if perhaps our street people and the homeless in the United States are allowing themselves to remain victims. Certainly mingling in the center is the position most Americans seem to lean toward. Not too rich, nor too poor. Not deathly ill, but never quite healthy. Not morally pure, but somewhere short of serious crime. And sooner or later we must step out in faith. We must lead, if only to become responsible for ourselves.

I fell asleep licking my cracked lips with a numb, dry,

parched tongue. It was difficult to tell if my light-headed-ness was from hunger, thirst, heat, or exhaustion.

We walked a second day under my leadership. Again the heat was severe. By now my throat was closing; it was becoming impossible for me to swallow. My tongue was so dry it was almost stiff, and it felt swollen several times the original size, a dry sponge between my teeth. Breathing was difficult. As I tried to force the hot air down further into my chest, I began to appreciate how these people had described the blessing they received shar-ing the nasal shape of the koala bear. Their broad expan-sive nose and large nasal passages were more adept at dealing with the soaring air temperature than my European pug nose.

The barren horizon grew more and more hostile. It seemed to defy humanity, to belong to something other than humans. The land had won all battles against progress, and now it seemed to regard life as alien. There were no roads, no airplanes overhead, not even the tracks of creatures could be seen.

I knew if the tribe did not help me soon, we would all certainly die. Our pace was slow, each step painfully forced. In the distance we could see a dark, heavily laden rain cloud. It tortured us by staying just far enough ahead so we could not walk fast enough and far enough to receive the bountiful gift it held. We could not even get close enough to share the benefit of the shadow. We could only see it in the distance and know that life-giving water was riding out in front of us like a carrot dangled before a donkey.

At one point I shouted. Perhaps to prove to myself I could, perhaps merely in desperation. But it was of no avail. The world merely swallowed up the sound like a ravished monster.

Cool water lay in wet pool mirages before my eyes, but when I arrived at the place in the sand, it was always only sand.

The second day passed without food, water, or help. That night I was too exhausted, ill, and discouraged to use even the pillow of hide; I think I passed out instead of going to sleep.

On the third morning I went to every individual in the group, and on my knees I begged as loudly as my dying body would permit, "Please help me. Please save us." It was very difficult to speak because I had awakened with my tongue so dry it was stuck fast to the inside of my cheek.

They listened and looked at me intently but only stood there smiling. I had the impression they were thinking, "We are hungry and thirsty too, but this is your experience, so we support you totally in what you must learn." No one offered any help.

We walked and walked. The air was still, the world totally inhospitable. It seemed to represent defiance against my intrusion. There was no help, no way out. My body was numb from the heat and had become unresponsive. I was dying. These were the signs of fatal dehydration. This was it. I was dying.

My thoughts jumped from subject to subject. I recalled my youth. Dad worked so hard all the time for the Santa Fe Railway. He was so handsome. There was never a time in my entire life he wasn't available to give love, support, and encouragement. Mom was always home for us. I remembered her feeding the hobos who knew magically, out of all the houses in town, the one where they were never refused. My sister was a straight-A student, so pretty and popular that I could watch her for hours dressing for a date. When I grew up I wanted to be just like my sister. In my mind I could picture my little brother, hugging our family dog and complaining about the girls at school wanting to hold his hand. As children, the three of us were very good friends. We would have stood by each other regardless of any circumstance. But over the years we had drifted apart. That day, I knew they would not even sense my desperation. I have read that when you are dying, your life flashes before you. My life wasn't exactly going through my brain like a video, but I was grasping at the strangest memories. I could picture myself standing in the kitchen drying dishes and studying spelling words. The most difficult word I ever wrestled with was air-conditioning. I could picture my falling in love with a sailor, and our church wedding, the miracle of birth, first my baby boy, and second, having my daughter born at home. I remembered all my jobs, schooling, degrees, education, then realized here I was dying in the Australian desert. What was it all about? Had I accomplished what my life was intended for? "Dear God," I said to myself. "Help me understand what is happening."

Instantly the answer came to me.

I had traveled over ten thousand miles from my American hometown, but I had not budged one inch in my thinking. I came from a left-brain world. I was raised on logic, judgment, reading, writing, math, cause and effect; here, I was in a right-brain reality, with people who used none of my so-called important educational concepts and civilized necessities. They were masters of the right brain, using creativity, imagination, intuition, and spiritual concepts. They didn't find it necessary to verbalize their communications; it was done through thought, prayer, meditation, whatever you might call it. I had begged and pleaded for help vocally. How ignorant I must have appeared to them. Any Real Person would have asked silently, mind to mind, heart to heart, individual to the universal consciousness that links all life together. I had up until that moment considered myself different, separate, apart from the Real People. They kept saying we are all One, and they live in nature as One, but until then I had been the observer. I had been keeping myself apart. I had to become One with them, with the universe, and communicate as the Real People did. So I did. Mentally I said "Thank you" to the source of this revelation, and in my mind I cried out, "Help me. Please, help me." I used the words I heard the tribe say each morning, "If it is in my highest good and the highest good for all of life everywhere, let me learn."

The thought came into my mind. "Put the rock in your mouth." I looked around. There were no rocks. We were walking on fine hour-glass sand. It came again. "Put the rock in your mouth." Then I remembered the rock I had chosen and still held in the cleavage of my chest. It had been there for months. I had forgotten it. I took it out and put it in my mouth, wallowed it around, and miraculously, moisture began to form. I could feel the ability to swallow being restored. There was hope. Perhaps I was not meant to die today.

"Thank you, Thank you, Thank you," I said in silence. I would have cried, but my body did not have enough moisture left for tears. So I continued mentally asking for help: "I can learn. I will do whatever is needed. Just help me find water. I don't know what to do, what to look for, where to walk."

The thought came to me: "Be water. Be water. When you can be water, you will find water." I didn't know what it meant. It didn't make sense. Be water! That isn't possible. But again I concentrated on forgetting my left-brain society programing. I shut out logic; I shut out reason. I opened myself up to intuition, and closing my eyes, I began being water. As I walked, I used all my senses. I could smell water, taste it, feel it, hear it, see it. I was cold, blue, clear, muddy, still, rippling, ice, melting, vapor, steam, rain, snow, wet, nourishing, splashing, expanding, unlimited. I was every possible image of water that came to mind.

We walked across a flat plain, level as far as the eye could see. There was only one small tawny mound in sight, a sand dune about six feet high with a rock ledge on top. It appeared misplaced in the bleak landscape. I walked up the side of it, my eyes half-closed in the blazing light, almost in a mental trance, and sat on the rock. I looked down, and there in front of me, all of my supportive, unconditionally-loving friends had stopped and were looking up with grins that spread across their faces from ear to ear. I faintly returned the smile. Then I stretched back my left hand to steady myself and felt something wet. My head jerked around. There behind me, in the continuation of the rock ledge I was perched on, was a rock pool about ten feet in diameter and about eighteen inches deep, filled with beautiful, crystal clear water from yesterday's taunting rain cloud.

I truly believe I was closer to our Creator with that first sip of tepid water than with any taste of communion I have ever received in a church.

Without a watch, I cannot be certain about the time, but I would estimate it took no more than thirty minutes from the time I started being water until we were putting our whole heads into the pool and shouting with joy.

While we were still celebrating our success, a giant reptile came walking by. It was enormous, something that looked like it was left over from prehistoric times. It was no illusion, but very real. Nothing could have been more appropriate to appear for dinner than this science-fiction-looking creature. The meat brought the euphoria that overwhelms people at feasts.

That night I understood for the first time the tribe's belief in the relationship of the land to characteristics of one's ancestors. Our giant, rocky cup seemed to burst through the flat surroundings and could easily be a nourishing breast of some past relative, her body consciousness now put into inorganic matter to save our lives. I privately christened the mound—Georgia Catherine, my mother's name.

I looked upward into the vast expanse of world surrounding us and, giving thanks, finally understood that the world is truly a place of abundance. It is full of kind, supporting people to share our lives if we let them. There is food and water for all beings everywhere if we are open to receiving and open to giving. But most of all I now appreciated the abundant spiritual guidance available in my life. Help was available in every stress, including a brush with death and the very act of dying, now that I had gotten past "doing it my way."

~~~~~~~~~~~~~~~~~~~~~~~~~~~

MY OATH

THERE WAS no differentiation in days of the week while living with the tribe. Nor was there any way of knowing in which month we were living. It was apparent that time was not an issue. One day I had the strangest feeling it was Christmas. Why, I'm not sure. There was nothing even remotely suggestive of a decorated pine tree or a crystal decanter of eggnog nearby. But, it probably was December 25. That made me think about days of the week and an incident that had happened in my office a few years prior.

In the waiting room were two Christian ministers who began discussing religion. The conversation seemed to ignite as they forcefully argued whether the true Sabbath, according to the Bible, was on Saturday or Sunday. Here in the Outback, my memory of the episode seemed comical. It was already the day after Christmas in New Zealand, and at this instant it was Christmas Eve in the

United States. I could picture the crooked red line I had
seen drawn through the blue ocean in the world atlas.
Time, it stated, started and stopped here. At an invisible
boundary on a constantly moving sea, every new day of
the week had its birth.

I also remembered, as a St. Agnes High School student,
sitting one Friday night on a stool at Allen's Drive-in. We
had whopper burgers before us and waited for the clock to
strike midnight. One bite of meat taken on Friday meant
instant mortal sin and eternal damnation. Years later the
rule was changed, but nobody ever answered my inquiry
into what happened to the poor damned souls already
convicted. Now it all seemed so stupid.

I could think of no greater way to honor the purpose
of Christmas than the way the Real People tribe live their
lives. They celebrate no holidays in our yearly manner.
They do honor each tribe member sometime throughout
the year, not on a specific birthday, but rather to acknowledge the person's talent, contribution to the community,
personal spiritual growth. They do not celebrate getting
older; what they do celebrate is becoming better.

One woman told me her name and talent in life meant
Time Keeper. They believe we are all multitalented and
progress through a series of strengths. She was presently
an artist of time and worked with another person who
had the ability of detailed memory recall. When I asked
her to explain further, she advised me the tribal members
were going to seek guidance about that, and I would be
told later if I was to have access to that knowledge or not.

There were about three nights when the conversation
was not interpreted for me. I knew without asking that
the discussion centered on the question of whether or not

to include me in some special information. I also knew it was not just me they were considering, but the fact that I represented all Mutants everywhere. It became apparent to me that the Elder was also doing a real sales pitch in my behalf on those three nights. I had the feeling Ooota was the one most opposed. I realized I had been chosen to have a unique experience no outsider had been allowed to have before. Perhaps the knowledge of timekeeping was asking too much.

We continued walking in the desert. The terrain was rock, sand, and some vegetation, hilly, and not as flat as most of what we had been through. There seemed to be a worn depression on the earth where generations of this black race had walked. Without warning, the group stopped and two men walked forward, parted bushes between two trees, and rolled boulders to one side. Behind them was an opening into the side of the hill. Sand had drifted up over the doorway; it was scooped away. Ooota turned to me and said:

> Now you are being allowed to know of time-keeping. Once you see, you will understand the dilemma my people have been going through. You cannot enter this sacred site until you give an oath that you will not reveal the whereabouts of this cave.

I was left alone on the outside as the others went in. I could smell smoke and see it faintly drifting upward from the rock covering the top of the hill. The people came to me one by one. First the youngest: he took my hands, looked into my eyes, and spoke in his native tongue, which I could not comprehend. I could sense his anxiety for what I would do with the knowledge I was about to receive. He was telling me with the inflection of his voice, the rhythm and pauses, that the welfare of his people was about to be exposed for the first time to a Mutant.

Next came the woman I knew as Story Teller. She, too, held my hands and talked to me. In the bright sun her face seemed blacker, her thin eyebrows blue-black, the shade of a peacock feather, and the whites of her eyes chalky clear. She motioned for Ooota to come and speak for us. He did, and while she held both of my hands and looked me squarely in the eyes, he relayed the words to me:

> The reason you have come to this continent is destiny. You made an agreement before birth to meet another and work together for your mutual benefit. The agreement was that you would not seek one another until at least fifty years had passed. Now is the time. You will know this person because you were both born in the same moment, and there is soul-level recognition. The pact was made on the very highest level of your eternal beingness.

I was shocked. The same information given to me when I first arrived in Australia by the strange young man in the tearoom was being repeated by this aging bush woman.

Next, Story Teller took a handful of sand and put it into my palm. Then she took another handful and opened her fingers and allowed the sand to filter through, indicating I should do the same. This was repeated four times in honor of the four factors: water, fire, air, and earth. A powdery residue clung to my fingers.

One by one they came outside, each speaking and holding my hands. But Ooota no longer spoke for them. After each one spent time with me they reentered the dwelling and someone else came out. Time Keeper herself was one of the last to come, and she was not alone. Memory Keeper was with her. They held hands so we became a threesome. We walked around in a circle, holding hands. Then we touched the ground with our fingers still clasped and later stood upright and stretched our hands into the sky. This was done seven times to honor the seven directions: north, south, east, west, above, below, and within.

Near the end, Medicine Man came. The Elder was last. Ooota accompanied him. They told me that the Aboriginal sacred sites, including those of the Real People tribe, no longer belonged to the natives. The most important joint tribal site was once *Uluru*, now called Ayers Rock, which is a gigantic red mound in the center of the country. It is the world's greatest monolith, standing 1,260 feet above the plain, and is now available to the tourists, who climb it like ants, then return to their excursion bus to spend the remainder of the day floating in the chlorinated, antiseptic swimming pools of the nearby motels. Even though the government says it is owned both by the British loyalists and the natives, it is obviously not sacred any longer and cannot be used for anything even remotely sacred. About 175 years ago, the Mutants began putting up telegraph lines across the vast open spaces. The natives had to find a different site for the gathering of the nations. Since then, all the art, historical carvings, and relics have been removed. Some of the objects were placed in Australian museums, but most of them were exported.

The graves have been robbed and altars stripped bare. The tribe believes Mutants were so insensitive that they assumed the Aboriginal worship would end when they took away the sacred sites. It never entered their minds that the people would go elsewhere. It was a devastating blow to all multitribal gatherings and was the beginning of what has developed into a total shattering of the Aboriginal nations. Some fought back and died in a losing battle. Most marched into the white man's world looking for the promised goodness, which included unlimited food, and died in poverty, the legal form of slavery.

The first white inhabitants of Australia were prisoners who arrived in chains by shiploads, to solve the overcrowding in the British penal system. Even the military sent to guard the offenders were men whom the royal courts considered expendable. It is no wonder that when a convict finished serving time and was released penniless and nonrehabilitated, he became a savage steward. The people over whom he could exercise power had to be persons lesser than himself. The natives filled this role.

Ooota revealed that his tribe was guided to come back here about twelve generations ago:

> This sacred place has kept our people alive since the beginning of time, when the land was full of trees, even when the great flood came that covered everything. Our people were safe here. It has not been detected by your airplanes, and your people cannot survive long enough in the desert to locate it. Very few humans know it exists. The ancient objects of our race have been taken by your people. We no longer have possession of

anything except what you will see here below the earth's surface. There is not another Aboriginal tribe that has any material objects left connected to their history. They have all been stolen by the Mutants. This is all that remains of an entire nation, an entire race, God's Real People. God's first people, the only true human beings left on the planet.

Healing Woman came to me a second time that afternoon. She carried a container of red paint. The colors they use represent, among other things, the four components of the body: bone, nerve, blood, and tissue. Her hand gesture and mental instructions told me to cover my face with red paint. I did. Then all the people came out, and again looking into each person's eyes, I agreed over and over never to reveal the exact location of this sacred site.

With that I was escorted in.

————————∞————————

23

DREAMTIME REVEALED

INSIDE WAS a mammoth room of solid rock walls with passageways leading off in several directions. Colorful banners adorned the walls, and statues jutted out from natural rock ledges. What I saw in the corner made me question my sanity. It was a garden! The rocks on the top of the hill are arranged so sunlight can enter, and I clearly heard the sound of water dripping on rock. There was underground water channeled through a rock trough that ran constantly the whole time we were there. It was an uncluttered atmosphere, simple but enduring.

This is the only time I ever saw any of the people claim what I would term personal possessions. In the cave, they kept their ceremonial supplies as well as more elaborate sleeping facilities, with many skins piled to make deep comfortable bedding. I recognized the camel hooves being made into cutting tools. I saw a room that I refer to as the museum. It was where they keep the stockpile of things collected over the years from the scouts who returned from the cities. There were magazine pictures of televisions, computers, automobiles, tanks, rocket launchers, slot machines, famous buildings, different races, and even gourmet food in glowing color. They also had objects that had been brought back to them—sunglasses, a razor, a belt, a zipper, safety pins, pliers, a thermometer, batteries, several pencils and pens, and a few books.

There was one section where they make a clothlike product. They trade wool and other fiber with neighboring tribes and sometimes make coverings out of tree bark. Rope is occasionally made here. I watched as one man, seated, took a few fibers in his hand and seemed to roll them on his thigh. Then, twisting, he continued to add fresh material until he had a long single thread. This was woven with other strands to form a rope of varying thickness. Hair is woven in many projects. I did not realize at the time that these people were covering their body because they knew it would be very difficult, perhaps even impossible, for me to deal with a clothesless lifestyle at this point in my life.

I spent the day in amazement, Ooota explaining as we explored. Torches were necessary in some areas further in, but all the main floor area had a rocky ceiling that allowed adjustment from outside and permitted light from dim to full brilliance. This cave of the Real People tribe is not a place of worship. In fact, their lives moment by moment are acts of worship. This most sacred site is where they can record history, and a place in which to teach Truth, to preserve values. It's a refuge from Mutant thought.

When we returned to the main chamber, Ooota held

the statues of wood and stone for my closer inspection.
His broad nostrils flaring, he explained that the head-
dresses revealed the statue's personality. A short headdress
represented head thoughts, our memory, decision making,
physical awareness of body senses, pleasures and pains,
all of which I related to conscious and subconscious mind.
The tall headdress represented our creative mind-self, how
we could tap into knowledge and invent yet-nonexisting
objects, have experiences that may or may not be real,
tune into the wisdom learned by all creatures and all
humans who ever lived. People seek information but do
not seem to realize that wisdom, too, seeks expression.
The tall headdress also represented our true perfect self,
the eternal part of each of us that we could turn to on
those occasions when we needed to know if an action we
were considering would be for our highest good. There
was also a third headdress, one that fanned the carved
face and draped down in back to touch the ground. This
represented the connection of all aspects: the physical, the
emotional, and the spiritual.

Most of the statues had incredible detail, but one, I
was surprised to see, had been finished without pupils in
the eyes. It looked like a sightless, blind symbol. "You
believe Divine Oneness sees and judges people," Ooota
said. "We think of Divine Oneness as feeling the intent
and the emotion of beings—not as interested in what we
do as why we do it."

That night was the most meaningful night of the
entire journey. It was then I learned why I was there and
what was expected of me.

We had a ceremony. I watched the artists prepare
paint of white pipe clay: two shades of red ochre and one

of lemon yellow. Tool Maker made paintbrushes out of short sticks about six inches long, frayed out and trimmed with his teeth. The people were painted with intricate designs and pictures of animals. They dressed me in a costume of feathers, some of which were from the soft vanilla-colored emu; I was to imitate the kookaburra bird. My scene in the ceremonial drama was to depict the bird as a messenger, flying to the far corners of the world. The kookaburra is a pretty bird, but it makes a loud noise, often compared to the braying of a donkey. The kookaburra has a strong sense of survival. It is a large bird and seemed appropriate to use.

After the singing and dancing concluded, we formed a small circle. There were nine of us: the Elder, Ooota, Medicine Man, Female Healer, Time Keeper, Memory Keeper, Peace Maker, Kin to Birds, and myself.

The Elder sat directly across from me, his legs tucked under him serving as a cushion; he leaned forward to look at me eye-to-eye. Someone outside the circle handed him a stone goblet filled with liquid. He took a sip. The penetrating stare into the depth of my heart did not waiver as he passed the cup to his right. He spoke:

We, the tribe of Divine Oneness Real People, are leaving planet Earth. In our remaining time we have elected to live the highest level of spiritual life: celibacy, a way to demonstrate physical discipline. We are having no more children. When our youngest member is gone, that will be the last of the pure human race.

We are eternal beings. There are many places in the universe where souls who are to follow us

can take on body forms. We are the direct descen-
dents of first beings. We have passed the test of
surviving since the beginning of time, holding
steadfast to the original values and laws. It is our
group consciousness that has held the earth
together. Now we have received permission to
leave. The people of the world have changed and
given a part of the soul of the land away. We go to
join it in the sky.

You have been chosen as our Mutant messenger to tell your kind we are going. We are leaving
Mother Earth to you. We pray you will see what
your way of life is doing to the water, the animals,
the air, and to each other. We pray you will find a
solution to your problems without destroying this
world. There are Mutants on the edge of regain-
ing their individual spirit of true beingness. With
enough focus, there is time to reverse the destruction on the planet, but we can no longer help you.
Our time is up. Already the rain pattern has been
changed, the heat is increased, and we have seen
years of plant and animal reproduction lessened.
We can no longer provide human forms for spirits
to inhabit because there will soon be no water or
food left here in the desert.

My mind was a whirl. Now it was making sense.
After all this time they had opened up to associate with an
outsider because they needed a messenger. But why me?

The cup of liquid was now mine. I took a sip. It had a
searing taste like vinegar mixed with straight whiskey. I
passed it on to the right.

The elder continued. "Now it is time to put your body and thoughts to rest. Sleep my sister; tomorrow we will speak again."

The fire had burned down to a glowing, red body of coals. Heat rose, escaping the cave through wide openings in the rocky ceiling. I could not sleep. I motioned to Peace Maker, asking if we could talk. He said, "Yes." Ooota agreed, so the three of us began a deep, complex conversation.

Peace Maker, his face as worn as the landscape we had traveled, told me that in the beginning of time, in what they call *dreamtime,* all earth was joined together. Divine Oneness created the light, the first sunrise shattering the total eternal darkness. The void was used to place many discs spinning in the heavens. Our planet was one of them. It was flat and featureless. There was not a hint of cover, the surface naked. All was silent. There was not a single flower to bend in air currents, nor was there even a breeze. No bird nor sound to penetrate the nonsound void. Then Divine Oneness expanded knowingness to each disc, giving different things to each one. The consciousness came first. From it appeared water, the atmosphere, land. All temporary forms of life were introduced. My people believe that what you call God, Mutants find difficult to define because they seem addicted to form. For us, Oneness has no size, shape, or weight. Oneness is essence, creativity, purity, love, unlimited, unbounded energy. Many of the tribal stories refer to a Rainbow Snake which represents the weaving line of energy or consciousness that starts as total peace, changes vibration, and becomes sound, color, and form.

I sensed it was not the consciousness of being awake or unconscious that Ooota was trying to explain, but rather some sort of creator consciousness. It is everything. It exists in rocks, plants, animals, and in humankind. Humans were created, but the human body only houses the eternal part of us. Other eternal beings are located in other places throughout the universe. Tribal belief says Divine Oneness first created the female, and that the world was sung into existence. Divine Oneness is not a person. It is God, a supreme, totally positive, loving power. It created the world by expanding energy.

They believe humans were made in the image of God, but not the physical image, because God has no body. Souls were made in the likeness of Divine Oneness, meaning they are capable of pure love and peace, and have the capacity for creativity and caretaking of many things. We were given free will and this planet to use as a learning place for emotions, which are uniquely acute when the soul is in human form.

Dreamtime has three parts, they told me. It was the time before time; dreamtime was also after land appeared but had yet no character. The early people, in experimenting with emotions and actions, found they had free will to feel angry if they so elected. They could look for things to feel angry about or create situations to make anger. Worry, greed, lust, lies, and power are not the feelings and emotions one should spend time developing. To illustrate that, early people disappeared, and in their place appeared a mass of rocks, a waterfall, or a cliff, or whatever. These things still exist in the world and are places of reflection for anyone wise enough to learn from them. It is consciousness that has formed the reality. The third part of dreamtime is *now.* The dreaming is still going on; consciousness is still creating our world.

That is one reason they don't believe ownership of land was ever intended. Land belongs to all things. Agreements and sharing are the real human way. Possession is the extreme of excluding others for self-indulgence. Before the British came, no one in Australia was without land.

The tribe believes the first earthly humans appeared in Australia when all the land on earth was joined. Scientists refer to a single landmass that existed about 180 million years ago as Pangea, and it ultimately split into two. Laurasis contained the northern continents, and Gondwanaland contained Australia, Antarctica, India, Africa, and South America. India and Africa drifted away 65 million years ago, leaving Antarctica below and Australia and South America between.

According to the tribe, early in the history of humankind, people began to explore and went on walkabouts further and further away. They encountered new situations and, instead of relying on basic principles, they adopted aggressive emotions and actions to survive. The further away they went, the more their belief system changed, the more their values were altered, and ultimately even their exterior evolved into a lighter color in the cooler northern climate.

They don't discriminate because of skin color, but they do believe we all started out the same shade and are heading back to one matching color.

They define Mutants as having specific characteristics. First, Mutants can no longer live in the open environment. Most die never knowing what it feels like to have stood naked in the rain. They spend their time in buildings with artificial heat and cooling, and suffer sunstroke out in the normal temperatures.

Secondly, Mutants no longer have the good digestive system of Real People. They have to pulverize, emulsify, process, and preserve food. They eat more unnatural things than natural ones. They have even gone so far as to develop allergies to basic foods and pollens in the air. Sometimes Mutant babies cannot even tolerate their own mother's milk.

Mutants have limited understanding because they measure time in terms of themselves. They fail to recognize any time except today and so destroy without regard for tomorrow.

But the big difference in humans now and the way they were originally is that Mutants have a core of fear. Real People have no fear. Mutants threaten their children. They need law enforcement and prisons. Even government security is based on threatening other countries with weapons. According to the tribe, fear is an emotion of the animal kingdom. There it plays an important part in the role of survival. But if humans know about Divine Oneness and understand that the universe is not a haphazard event but is an unfolding plan, they cannot be fearful. You either have faith or fear, not both. Things, they think, generate fear. The more things you have, the more you have to fear. Eventually you are living your life for things.

The Real People explained how absurd it appeared to them when the missionaries insisted they teach their children to fold hands and give two minutes of grace before meals. They wake up being grateful! They spend the entire day never taking anything for granted. If missionaries have to teach their own children to be grateful, something that comes innately to all humans, the tribe feels they should take a very serious look at their own society. Perhaps it is they who need help.

They also can not understand why the missionaries forbid their payments to the earth. Everyone knows, the less you take from the land, the less you owe in return. The Real People see nothing savage in paying a debt or showing your gratitude to the earth by letting some of your own blood spill onto the sand. Also, they believe in honoring the individual desire of a person who wishes to stop nourishment and sit in the open to end their worldly existence. They do not believe that death by disease or accident is natural. After all, they said, you can't really kill something eternal. You did not create it, and you can't kill it. They believe in free will; freely the soul chooses to come, so how can rules be just that say the soul cannot go home? It is not a personality decision made in this manifested reality. It is an eternal-level decision that is made by an all-knowing self.

They believe the natural way to exit the human experience is by exercising one's free will and choice. At about age 120 or 130, when a person gets excited about returning to *forever,* and after asking Oneness if it is in the highest good, they call for a party, a celebration of their life.

The Real People nation have for centuries had the practice at birth of speaking the same first phrase to all newborns. Each person hears the same exact first human words: "We love you and support you on the journey." At their final celebration, everyone hugs them and repeats this phrase again. What you heard when you came is what you hear when you leave! Then the departing person sits down in the sand and shuts down the body systems. In less than two minutes they are gone. There is no sorrow or mourning. They agreed to teach me their technique for transforming from the human plane back to the invisible plane when I was ready for the responsibility of such knowledge.

The word *Mutant* seems to be a state of heart and head, not a color or a person; it is an attitude! It is someone who has lost or closed off ancient remembering and universal truths.

Finally we had to conclude our discussion. It was very late, and we were all exhausted. This cave was empty yesterday, and now it was filled with life. My brain held years of education yesterday, but now it seemed a sponge for different and more important knowledge. Their way of life was so foreign and so deep for me to comprehend that I was grateful when my thinking process fell into a veneer of peaceful unconsciousness.

24

~~~~~~~~~~~~~~~~~~~~~~

ARCHIVES

THE FOLLOWING morning I was allowed to see the passage they call Timekeeping. They have created a stone device that allows the sun to shine down a shaft. There is only one time a year that it shines in a direct and exact pattern. When it does, they know that a full year has passed since the last recorded time. At that time, a great celebration honoring the woman called Time Keeper and the woman called Memory Keeper takes place. The two archivists then perform their annual ritual. They create a mural on the wall of all the significant activities for the past six Aboriginal seasons. All births and deaths are recorded by day of the season and time of the sun or moon, as well as other important observations. I counted over 160 of these carvings and paintings. That is how I determined the youngest tribal member to be thirteen and that we had four people in the group over ninety.

I was unaware that the Australian government had

ever participated in any nuclear activity until I saw it indicated on the cave wall. The government probably had no
idea there were any humans around the test site. They
have the bombing of Darwin by the Japanese recorded on
the wall. Without the use of pencil or paper, Memory
Keeper knew each important event in the proper sequence
it was to be recorded. When Time Keeper described their
responsibility of chiseling and painting, her expression
turned to such delight it was like looking into the eyes of
a child who has just received a treasured gift. Both of
these women are of advanced age. I was amazed how our
culture is filled with elderly citizens who are forgetful,
unresponsive, unreliable, and senile, while here in the wild
as people get older, the wiser they become, and they are
valued for their input into discussions. They are pillars of
strength and examples for the others.

I counted back and found the carving on the wall that
depicted the year of my birth. There in the season that
reflected September, what would be our twenty-ninth day,
in the early morning hours, a birth was recorded. I asked
who the individual was. I was told it was Regal Black
Swan, now known as the Tribal Elder.

My mouth probably did not drop open in astonish-
ment, but it easily could have. What are the chances of
meeting someone else who is born the same day, same
year, and same hour, on the opposite end of the earth, and
having the knowledge foretold? I told Ooota I wanted to
speak privately with Regal Black Swan. He arranged it.

Years before, Black Swan had been told of a spiritual
partner who inhabited a personality born on the top of
the globe in the society of Mutants. As a youth, he wanted
to venture into the Australian society to seek such a per-

son but was told that the agreement of allowing each partner at least fifty years to develop values should be honored.

We compared our births. His life began as his mother, alone, after traveling many days to a specific location, hand-dug and squatted over a sandpit lined in the ultra-soft fur of a rare albino koala. Mine began in a white, sterile hospital in Iowa after my mother, too, traveled many miles from Chicago to a specific location of her choice. His father was traveling and miles away when the birth took place. So was mine. In his lifetime so far, he had changed his name several times. So had I. He told the circumstances of each change. The rare, white koala who had appeared on the path of his mother was the indication that the spirit of the child she carried was destined for leadership. He personally had experienced the kinship to the Australian black swan and later combined the swan with the adornment of their word, translated for me into Regal. I told him the circumstances of my name changes.

It didn't really matter if our connection was myth or fact. It became a partnership in reality at that very instant. We had many heart-to-heart talks.

Most of what we talked about was personal and would not be appropriate in this manuscript, but I will share with you what I feel was his most profound statement.

Regal Black Swan told me that in this world of personalities, there is always a duality. I had interpreted it as good versus bad, slavery or freedom, conformity and its opposite. But that is not the case. It is not black or white; it is always shades of gray. And most important, all the gray is moving in a progressive pattern back to the originator. I teased about our age and told him I needed another fifty years just for comprehension.

Later the same day, in the Timekeeping passage, I learned the Aborigines are the original inventors of spray paint. In keeping with their deep concern for the environment, they use no toxic chemicals; they have refused to change with the times, so the method of choice in the year 1000 is still the choice today. They painted an area on the wall in deep red, using fingers and a brush of animal hair. A few hours later it had dried, and I was instructed how to mix white paint from chalky clay, water, and lizard oil. We used a flat piece of bark to combine the mixture. When it appeared to be of acceptable consistency, they folded the bark into a funnel and I poured the paint in my mouth. It was a strange sensation on my tongue but had very little taste. Next, I placed my hand on the red wall and began to spit the paint out all around my fingers. Finally I lifted my spattered hand, and there was the mark of the Mutant on the sacred wall. I could not have been more highly honored if my face were plastered on the ceiling of the Sistine Chapel.

I spent one entire day studying the wall data. There was acknowledgment of the ruler of England, of the exchange of money being introduced, the first sighting of a car, an airplane, the first jet, the satellites circling over Australia, eclipses, even what appeared to be a flying saucer vehicle with Mutants that looked more mutated than I! Some of the things I was told were eyewitness accounts by the previous Time Keepers and Memory Keepers, but others were reported events brought back by observers sent to the civilized areas.

They used to send young people but learned it was

too difficult a task for youth. The young were easily impressed by the promise of owning a pickup truck, being able to eat ice cream every day, and having access to all the wonders of the industrial world. Older people were more grounded and acknowledged the pull of the magnet but did not succumb. However, no one was ever held to the tribal family against their choice; periodically a lost member returned. Ooota had been taken from his mother at birth which was not only common in the past but was lawful. In order to convert pagans and save their souls, children were put into institutions and forbidden to learn their native languages or practice any sacred rites. Ooota was reared for sixteen years in the city before he ran away to find his roots.

We all laughed when Ooota told how the government sometimes provided housing for the Aborigines. The people slept in the yard and used the house for storage. That brought up their definition of a gift. According to the tribe, a gift is only a gift when you give someone what the person wants. It is not a gift if you give what you want them to have. A gift has no attachment. It is given unconditionally. The persons receiving it have the right to do anything with the gift: use it, destroy it, give it away, whatever. It is theirs without condition, and the giver expects nothing in return. If it doesn't fit that criteria, it is not a gift. It should be classified as something else. I had to agree that government gifts and, unfortunately, most of what my society would consider a gift would be classified differently by these people. But, too, I could remember several people back home who give gifts constantly and aren't aware of it. They give words of encouragement, share humorous incidents, offer others a shoulder to lean on, or are simply unfailing friends.

The wisdom of these people was a constant source of amazement to me. If only they were the world leaders, what a difference there would be in our relationships!

25

~~~~~~~~~~~~~~~~~~~~~~~~~

COMMISSIONED

THE FOLLOWING day I was allowed to enter the most protected floor space in this underground site. It was the area held in the highest regard and the center of most of the previous discussion regarding my questionable admittance. We had to use torches to light the room of polished, inset opal. The light from the fire reflecting off the walls, floor, and ceiling was perhaps the most brilliant display of rainbow color I have ever witnessed. I felt I was standing inside a crystal with dancing colors under me, over me, and hugging my sides. This room was where people went formally to communicate directly with Oneness, in what we might call meditation. They explained to me that the difference between Mutants' prayer and the Real People form of communication is that prayer is an outward talking to the spiritual world, and what they do is just the opposite. They listen. They clear thoughts out of their minds and wait to receive. The reasoning seemed to be, "You cannot hear the voice of Oneness when you are busy talking."

In this room many marriage ceremonies have been held and names have been officially changed. It is often the place older members want to visit when they are dying. In the past, when this race was the sole occupant of the continent, different clans used different methods of burial. Some buried their dead wrapped in mummy fashion, in tombs cut into sides of the mountains. Ayers Rock at one time had many bodies, but now, of course, all that is gone. The people don't really put much significance in the dead human body, so it was often buried in a shallow sandpit. They believe it is proper that it should ultimately return to the soil to be recycled, as all elements in the universe are. Some natives now request to be left uncovered in the desert, becoming food for the animal kingdom that has so faithfully provided nourishment in the cycle of all life. The big difference, as my understanding provided, is that Real People know where they are going when they draw their last earthly breath and most Mutants don't. If you know, you leave peacefully and confidently; if you don't, there is obviously a struggle.

Very special teaching also takes place within the jeweled chamber. It is a classroom where the art of disappearing is taught. The Aboriginal race has long been rumored to vanish into thin air when confronted with danger. Many of the urban-dwelling natives say it was always a hoax. Their people were never able to do superhuman feats. But they are wrong. The art of illusion is being performed on master levels out here in the desert. The Real People also know how to perform the illusion of multiplication. One person can seem to be ten or fifty. It is used instead of a weapon to survive. They capitalize on the fear possessed by other races. It isn't necessary to spear them for elimination; they merely provide illusions of mass power, and the fear-filled individuals run screaming, later telling tales of devils and evil sorcery.

We stayed at the sacred site for only a few days, but before we left I was given a ceremony in the sacred room that made me their spokesperson, and they performed a special rite to assure my future protection. The ritual began by anointing my head. A circle of swirled silver-gray koala fur, with a polished opal set in resin in the center, was attached above my forehead. I had feathers glued all over my body, including my face. Everyone wore feather costumes. It was a wonderful celebration in which they used wind chimes operated from waving fans made of feathers and reeds. The sound was as incredible as organs I have heard in the world's finest cathedrals. They also used clay pipes and a short wooden instrument that sounded much like our flutes.

I knew then I had been truly accepted. I had passed the tests they had given me, although I wasn't informed beforehand that I was being tested, nor did I know the purpose. Being in the center of their circle, being sung to, and listening to the ancient, pure sounds of their music, I was very, very deeply moved.

The next morning, only a portion of the original group left the secret place to accompany me on the continuation of our journey. To where? I did not know.

26

-~~~~~~~~~~~~~~~~~~~~~~~~~-

HAPPY UNBIRTHDAY

DURING OUR journey there were two occasions that we celebrated by honoring someone's talent. Everyone is recognized by a special party, but it has nothing to do with age or birthdate—it is in recognition of uniqueness and contribution to life. They believe that the purpose for the passage of time is to allow a person to become better, wiser, to express more and more of one's beingness. So if you are a better person this year than last, and only you know that for certain, then you call for the party. When you say you are ready, everyone honors that.

One of the celebrations we had was for a woman whose talent, or medicine, in life was being a listener. Her name was Secret Keeper. No matter what anyone wanted to talk about, get off their chest, confess, or vent, she was always available. She considered the conversations private, didn't really offer advice, nor did she judge. She held the person's hand or held their head in her lap and just listened. She seemed to have a way of encouraging people to find their own solutions, to follow what their hearts were directing them to do.

I thought of people at home in the United States: the number of young people who seemed to have no sense of direction or purpose, the homeless people who think they have nothing to offer society, the addicted individuals who want to function in some reality other than the one we are in. I wished I could bring them here, to witness how little it takes, sometimes, to be a benefit to your community, and how wonderful it is to know and experience a sense of self-worth.

This woman knew her strong points and so did everyone else. The party consisted of Secret Keeper, sitting slightly elevated, and the rest of us. She had requested that the universe provide bright foods, if that was in order. Sure enough, that evening we found ourselves walking in plants that held berries and grapes.

We had seen a rainfall in the distance some days before, and we found scores of tadpoles in small pools of water. The tadpoles were laid upon the hot rocks and quickly dried into another form of food I had never dreamed possible. Our party menu also included some type of unattractive mud-hopping creature.

At the party we had music. I taught the Real People a Texas line dance, Cotton-Eyed Joe, which we modified to their drumbeat, and before long we were all laughing. Then I explained how Mutants like to dance with partners and asked Regal Black Swan to join me. He learned waltz steps immediately, but we couldn't get the beat just right. I started humming the tune and encouraged them to join me. Before long we had the group humming and waltzing under the Australian sky. I also showed them how to square dance. Ooota did a great job as the caller. That night they decided that perhaps I had already mastered the art of healing in my society and might wish to go into the music field!

It was the closest I ever got to receiving an Aborigine name. They felt I had more than one talent and were discovering that I could love them and their way of looking at life as well as remaining loyal to my own, so they nicknamed me Two Hearts.

At Secret Keeper's party, various people took turns telling what a comfort it was to have her in the community and how valuable her work was for everyone. She glowed humbly and took the praise in a dignified and royal manner.

It was a great night. As I was falling asleep, I said, "Thank you" to the universe for such a remarkable day.

I would not have agreed to come with these people had I been given the choice. I would not order tadpole to eat if it were on a menu; and yet I was remembering how meaningless some of our holidays have become and how wonderful these times were.

27

WIPED OUT

THE GROUND ahead of us was riveted by erosion. Ravines
ten feet deep kept us from walking in a straight direction.
Suddenly the sky became dark. Voluminous gray thunder
clouds were above us, and we could see the rolling activity taking place in the sky. Lightning struck the ground
only a few feet away. It was followed by a deafening
crack. The sky became a ceiling of strobed flashes.
Everyone ran for cover. Although we scattered in all directions, no one seemed to locate any actual shelter. The terrain in that part of the country was somewhat less barren.
There were scrub bushes, a few sparse and struggling
trees, and a form of brittle ground cover.

We could see the cloudburst and rain being driven in a
slant toward the ground. I could hear it in the distance,
like a rumbling train approaching. The ground gave a
tremor under my feet. Giant drops of water fell from the
heavens. Lightning struck and the claps of thunder were

loud enough to stir my nervous system to attention. I instantly searched for the thong around my waist. I was carrying a water vessel and, a dilly bag made from goanna, stocked by Female Healer with many of her grasses, oils, and powders. She had carefully explained where each had originated and their purpose, but I realized her form of treatment would realistically take as long to learn and master as our American six-year healing arts programs to become an M.D., D.C., or D.O. I felt the knot to make sure it was secure.

Through all the noise and activity I was aware of hearing something else, something very powerful, something new, an aggressive sound with which I was not familiar. Ooota shouted to me, "Grab a tree! Hold tight to a tree!" There were none close by. I looked up and saw something rolling across the desert floor. It was tall, black, and thirty feet wide, and it was traveling very fast! It was upon me before I had a chance to reason. Water, a flood of swirling, muddy, foaming water covered my head. My whole body twisted and turned in the avalanche. I struggled for air. My hands clawed out, trying to grab something, anything. I had no sense of up or down. Mud, heavy mud, filled my ears. My body tumbled, doing somersaults. I came to a stop as my side struck something solid, very solid. I was pinned, wrapped around a bush. Reaching with my head and neck as far as it would stretch, I gasped for air. My lungs screamed for oxygen. I had to inhale. I had no choice, even if I was still under water. The terror I felt was beyond telling. It seemed I must surrender to forces I could not even comprehend. Prepared to drown, my gasp received air, not water. I couldn't open my eyes; there was too much weight from the mud on my face. I felt the bush pushing into my side as the power of the water forced me to bend more and more.

As quickly as it had come, it was over. The wave rolled past, the water behind it steadily decreasing. I could feel big raindrops on my skin. I turned my face upward and let the rain erode the mud from my eyes. I tried to straighten up and felt myself drop slightly. Finally I tried opening my eyes. Looking around, I saw my legs dangling about five feet above the ground. I was midway down on the side of the ravine. I heard voices of the others beginning to emerge. I couldn't climb up, so I let myself drop to the bottom. My knees took the brunt of the shock, and I began to stagger down the ravine. I soon realized the voices were coming from the opposite direction, so I turned around.

Before long we were all reunited. No one had received any serious injury. Our load of sleeping skins was gone, as was my waist belt and the precious cargo. We stood in the rain and let the mud caked on our bodies return to Mother Earth. One by one the people removed the cloths around them, stood naked, and let the grit from the creases and folds of the fabric wash away. I took mine off too. I had lost my headband in the underwater ballet, so I ran my fingers through the matted mess of hair on my head. It must have looked like fun because the others came to help. Several of the pieces of clothing we had laid upon the ground had collected rainwater. They motioned for me to sit, and when I did they began pouring the water through my hair and separating the strands with their fingers.

When the rain stopped, we put our cloths back on.

Finally dried, we just brushed the remaining sand from them. The hot air seemed to lap up the moisture, leaving my skin like stretched canvas on an easel. It was at this point I was told the tribe prefers not to wear clothing in extreme heat, but because they felt I might be too emotionally uncomfortable, as a gesture of being my hosts and hostesses they observed my ways.

The truly amazing thing about the whole episode was the short duration of stress it created. Everything was gone, but in no time the people had us all laughing. I admitted I felt and probably looked better as a result of my flash-flood sponging. This storm had shocked my awareness of the magnitude of life and my passion for it. This brush with death also stripped my belief that things outside of myself were causes for joy or despair. Literally, everything except the rags around our bodies had been swept away. The small gifts I had received, things I would have carried back to the United States and passed on to my grandchildren, were destroyed. The choice was presented—to respond by lamenting or by acceptance. Was it a fair exchange—my only material possessions for the instant lesson on nonattachment? I was told that I probably would have been allowed to retain the keepsakes that had been swept away, but in the energy of Divine Oneness, I apparently was still feeling too much attachment and importance to them. Had I finally learned to treasure the experience and not the item?

That evening they dug a small hole in the earth. A fire was made in it and several stones were placed so they became extremely hot. When the fire had burned out and only the rock remained, moist twigs were added, then thick root vegetables, and finally dry grass. The pit was closed with additional sand. We waited, almost like one waits for baked goods in a General Electric oven. After about an hour, we unearthed the food and gratefully ate the marvelous meal.

As I fell asleep that night, minus the comfort of any dingo hide, the famous serenity prayer came into my mind: "God grant me the serenity to accept the things I cannot change, the courage to change the things I can, and the wisdom to know the difference."

28

~~~~~~~~~~~~~~~~~~~~~~~~~~~~~

BAPTISM

AFTER THE torrential rain, the flowers appeared out of nowhere. The landscape went from barren nothingness to a carpet of color. We walked on flowers, ate them, and wore garlands of flowers all over our bodies. It was wonderful.

We were getting closer to the coast, with the desert behind us. Each day the vegetation became more dense. The plants and trees were taller and more numerous. Food was more abundant. There was a whole new variety of seeds, sprouts, nuts, and wild fruits. One man cut a small indentation into a tree. We held our newly acquired water vessels next to this opening, and I watched the water funnel directly from the tree into the container. We had our first opportunity to catch fish. The smoked flavor still lingers as a precious memory in my mind. We had access to numerous eggs, both reptile and bird.

One day we came to a magnificent pool in the wilderness. They had been teasing me all day about having a special surprise, and it certainly was. The water was cold and deep. The large pool lay in a rocky stream basin with lots of dense brush around it, almost a jungle atmosphere. I was very excited, as my fellow travelers knew I would be. It looked big enough for taking a good swim, so I asked permission to do so. They told me to be patient. The permission would either be granted or declined by the inhabitants who ruled this territory. The tribe went through a ritual of asking to share the pool. While they were chanting, the top of the water began to ripple. It seemed to start in the center and move toward the bank opposite of where we were standing. Then a long, flat head appeared, followed by the rough exterior of a six-foot crocodile. I had forgotten about crocodiles. There was one more called to the surface, then both crawled out of the water and into the surrounding foliage. When I was told it was okay to swim, my original enthusiasm had dampened.

"Are you sure they are all out?" I questioned mentally. How could they know for certain there were only two? They assured me by taking a long tree branch and probing the water. Nothing responded from the deep. A sentry was stationed to watch for the crocs to return, and we went swimming. It was refreshing to splash in the water and to float, my spine totally relaxed for the first time in ages.

As strange as it probably sounds, somehow, my submerging fearlessly into the crocodile pool was symbolic of another baptism in this lifetime. I had not found a new religion, but I had found new faith.

We did not camp near the pool but continued our

journey that day. The second time we encountered a crocodile it was much smaller and appeared in the manner I now recognized as providing us with life, by volunteering to be dinner. The Real People don't eat much crocodile meat. They feel the reptile has an aggressive and cunning behavior. The vibration from the meat can mix with personal vibrations, causing the person to have more difficulty remaining peaceful and nonviolent. We had baked crocodile eggs which tasted horrible. However, when you request the universe to provide dinner, you don't second-guess what arrives. You just know in the big picture that all is in order, so you go with the flow, swallow large gulps, and decline second helpings!

While traveling along the waterway, we found numerous water snakes. They were kept alive so we would have fresh meat for dinner. At the campsite I watched as several people held the snakes firmly and put a hissing head into their mouth. Gripping the snake head firmly with their teeth, they moved their hands and with a strong, sudden thrust brought instant painless death in honor of this creature's purpose of existence. I knew they believed strongly that Divine Oneness planned no suffering to any living creature, except what the creature accepts for itself. That applied to humanity as well as animals. While the snakes were being smoked, I sat smiling, thinking of an old friend, Dr. Carl Cleveland, and his years of emphasizing precision movement when he taught students to reset joints. Someday, I reminded myself, I would share this moment's activity with him.

"There should be no suffering by any creature except what they accept for themselves." That was a thought to ponder. Spirit Woman explained that each individual soul on the highest level of our being could, and sometimes did, select to be born into an imperfect body; they often came to teach and influence the lives they touched. Spirit Woman said that members of the tribe who had been murdered in the past had selected prior to birth to live their life to the fullest but, at some point in time, to be a part of some other soul's enlightenment test. If they were killed, it was with their agreement on an eternal level and only indicated how truly they understood *forever.* It meant the murderer had failed the challenge and would be tested again someplace in the future. All diseases and disorders, they believe, have some spiritual connection and serve as stepping-stones if Mutants would only open up and listen to their bodies to learn what is taking place.

That night in a black and featureless desert, I heard the world come alive, and I realized I had finally overcome my fear. Perhaps I started as a reluctant urban student, but it now seemed right for me to have this experience here in the Outback where only earth, sky, and ancient life exists, where prehistoric scales, fangs, and claws are ever present, yet are dominated by fearless people.

I felt I was finally ready to face the life I had apparently chosen to inherit.

29

RELEASED

We HAD been climbing and made camp on ground much higher than our previous altitude. The air was fresh and crisp, and they told me that, sight unseen, the ocean was not far away.

It was very early in the morning. The sun had not yet risen, but many people were already stirring. They prepared a morning fire, which was rare. I looked up and saw the falcon perched above me in a tree.

We had the usual morning ritual and then Regal Black Swan took my hand and brought me closer to the fire. Ooota told me the Elder wanted to say a special blessing. Everyone gathered around; I stood in a circle of outstretched arms. All eyes were closed and faces pointed skyward. Regal Black Swan spoke to the heavens. Ooota spoke to me:

"Hello, Divine Oneness. We stand here before you with a Mutant. We have walked with her and know that she contains yet a spark of your perfection. We have touched her and changed her, but transforming a Mutant is a very difficult task.

"You will see that her strange pale skin is becoming more naturally brown, and her white hair is growing away from her head where beautiful dark hair has taken root. But, we have not been able to influence the odd-colored eyes.

"We have taught the Mutant much, and we have learned from her. It seems Mutants have something in their life called gravy. They know truth, but it is buried under thickening and spices of convenience, materialism, insecurity, and fear. They also have something in their lives called frosting. It seems to represent how they spend almost all the seconds of their existence in doing superficial, artificial, temporary, pleasant-tasting, nice-appearing projects and spend very few actual seconds of their lives developing their eternal beingness.

"We have chosen this Mutant, and we release her as a bird from the edge of a nest, to fly away, far and high, and to screech like the kookaburra, telling the listeners that we are leaving.

"We do not judge the Mutants. We pray for them and release them as we pray and release ourselves. We pray they will look closely at their actions, at their values, and learn before it is too late that all life is one. We pray they will stop the destruction of the earth and of each other. We pray there are enough Mutants on the brink of becoming real to change things.

"We pray the Mutant world will hear and accept our messenger.

"End of message."

Spirit Woman walked with me some distance and, as the sun was beginning to break through the dawn, she pointed to the city spread out before us. It was time for my return to civilization. Her wrinkled brown face and piercing black eyes looked out beyond the cliff edge. She spoke in her blunt native language, pointing to the distant city, and I understood this was to be a morning of release—the tribe releasing me, and my letting go of the teachers. How well had I learned their lessons? Only time would tell. Could I remember it all? It was funny, I was more concerned about delivering their message than I was about my reentry into the Aussie society.

We returned to the group and each of the tribal members said good-bye. We exchanged what seems to be a universal form of farewell among true friends—a hug. Ooota said, "There was nothing we could give you that you did not already have, but we feel even though we could not give to you, you learned to accept, receive, and take from us. That is our gift." Regal Black Swan took hold of my hands. I think he had tears in his eyes. I know I did. "Please do not ever lose your two hearts, my friend," he said, as Ooota interpreted for us. "You came to us with two open hearts. Now they are filled with understanding and emotion for both our world and your own. You have given me the gift of a second heart also. I now have knowledge and understanding that is beyond anything I could have imagined for myself. I treasure our friendship. Go in peace, with our thoughts for your protection."

His eyes seemed lighted from within as he thoughtfully added, "We shall meet again, without our cumbersome human bodies."

30

HAPPY ENDING?

As I walked away, I knew my life would never again be as simple and as meaningful as it had been these last few months, and that a part of me would always wish it could return.

It took me most of the day to walk the distance into the city. I had no idea how I would handle getting from this place, wherever it was, back to my rental house. I could see the highway but didn't think it would be a very good idea to walk along it, so I continued through the bush. At one point I turned around to look back, and just then a gust of wind came out of nowhere. Like a giant eraser my footprints were wiped from the sand. It seemed to clean the slate of my existence in the Outback. My periodic overseer, the brown falcon, swooped over my head just as I came to the edge of the city.

There was an elderly man in the distance. He wore blue jeans, a sports shirt tucked in his thick-belted midline, and an old, well-worn, green bush hat. He did not smile as I approached; instead, his eyes widened in disbelief.

Yesterday I had everything I needed: food, clothing, shelter, health care, companions, music, entertainment, support, a family, and lots of joyful laughter—all free. But that world was now gone.

Today, unless I begged for money, I could not function. Everything required to exist had to be purchased. I had no options; I was at this moment reduced to a filthy, tattered beggar. I was a bag lady without even a bag. Only I knew the truth of the person contained within this exterior of poverty and grime. My relationship with the world's homeless was in that instant forever changed.

Approaching the Australian man, I asked, "May I borrow some change? I just came out of the bush and must make a telephone call. I have no money. If you will give me your name and address, I will repay you."

He just continued to stare, so intently that the lines on his brow changed direction. Then he reached into his right-hand pocket, extracting the coin, while he held his nostrils closed with his left hand. I knew I had offensive body odor again. It had been about two weeks since my soapless bath in the crocodile pool. He shook his head, not interested in being repaid, and quickly walked away.

I wandered down a few streets and saw some schoolchildren gathered together. They stood awaiting the arrival of afternoon transportation home. All had the scrubbed-clean appearance typical of Australian uniform-clad youth, their clothing all identical. Only the shoes showed any sign of individual expression. They stared at my bare feet, now looking more like a hoofed mutation than a human female appendage.

I knew I looked dreadful and only hoped my appearance was not too frightening, with the scant clothing and my hair uncombed for over 120 days. The skin on my face, shoulders, and arms had peeled so often I was freckled and blotched. Besides that, I had already received confirmation that, quite bluntly, I stank!

"Excuse me," I said. "I just came out of the bush. Can you tell me where I can find a telephone, and would any of you happen to know where the telegraph office is located?"

Their reaction was reassuring. They were not frightened, only filled with giggles and laughter. My American accent served as further foundation to the basic Aussie belief: All Americans are odd. I was advised there was a phone box two blocks away.

I called my office and asked them to wire money, and they gave me the address for the telegraph company. I walked there, and from the expressions on their faces as I arrived, they had been told to look for someone with a very unusual appearance. The clerk reluctantly released the funds to me without the required identification. As I picked up the stack of bills, she sprayed both the counter and me with a Lysol-type spray.

With money in hand I took a taxi to a large discount store and purchased slacks, shirt, rubber thongs, shampoo, hairbrush, toothpaste, toothbrush, and bobby pins. The cab driver stopped at an outdoor market, where I loaded a plastic bag with fresh fruit and bought a half dozen different kinds of juices in throwaway cartons. Then he drove me to a motel and waited until I was accepted. We both questioned if they would let me in, but money in hand seems to speak louder than questionable appearance. I turned on the bathwater and blessed the bathtub. While it filled, I called the airlines for a flight out the following day. The next three hours I spent soaking in the tub, sorting out the details of the last few years, and especially the last few months of my life.

The next day I boarded a plane, face scrubbed, hair ugly but clean, hobbling on the thongs which I had to cut and barely fit over the acquired hoof, but I smelled wonderful! I had forgotten to buy clothes with pockets, so my money was stuffed inside the shirt.

The landlady was glad to see me. I was right, she had covered with the property owners while I was gone. No problem—I just owed back payments. The wonderfully friendly Australian business owner who leased me the television and video recorder just before I left had not even sent a notice or tried to repossess his equipment. He, too, was glad to see me. He knew I wouldn't leave without returning his merchandise and settling the bill. My project was still there awaiting my attention. The healthcare participants were upset but joked and asked if I had gone opal mining instead of coming back to the office. I learned that the owner of the jeep had agreed that if Ooota and I did not return, he was to go into the desert for his vehicle and then call my employer. He told them I had gone on walkabout, which meant destination unknown and traveling on Aboriginal nontime. They had no choice but to accept my actions. No one else could complete the project, so it was still there waiting for me.

I called my daughter. She was relieved and excited to hear everything that had happened and confessed she never had a feeling of uneasiness about my disappearance. She was certain that if I had been in serious trouble, she would have sensed it somehow. I opened my accumulated mail and learned I had been dropped from the family Christmas exchange by the relative in charge! There were no excuses for not sending them Christmas gifts.

It took time soaking, using a pumice stone, and applying lotion to make my feet receptive to hose and shoes once again. At one point I used an electric knife to saw off most of the dead tissue!

I found myself being grateful for the oddest items, such as the razor that removed the growth of hair under my arms, the mattress that elevated me above miniscule jaws, a roll of toilet paper. I tried, over and over, to tell people about the tribe I had grown to love. I tried to explain about their way of life, their value system, and most of all their message of concern about the planet. Every time I read something new in the paper about the seriousness of environmental damage and the predictions of how the greenest and most lush vegetations may be burned into nonexistence, I knew it was right; the Real People tribe had to leave. They could barely function on the food available now, let alone deal with future radiation effects. They were correct that humans cannot make oxygen. Only the trees and plants can do that. In their words, "We are destroying the soul of the earth." Our technical greed has uncovered a deep ignorance that is a serious threat to all life, an ignorance that only reverence for nature can reverse. The Real People tribe have earned the right not to continue their race on this already over-populated plant. Since the beginning of time they have remained truthful, honest, peaceful people who have never doubted their connection with the universe.

The part I did not understand was that no one I spoke

184 MUTANT MESSAGE DOWN UNDER

to was interested in the values of the Real People. I realized that to grasp the unknown, to embrace what looks different was threatening. But I tried to explain that it may expand our awareness; it might cure our social problems; it may even cure disease. It fell on deaf ears. The Australians became defensive. Even Geoff, who had at one point hinted about marriage, could not accept the possibility that wisdom could come from bush people. He implied it was great I had experienced a once-in-a-lifetime adventure and now hoped I could settle down and accept the expected female role. Eventually I left Australia, my health-care project completed, my Real People story untold.

It seemed the next leg of my journey in life was not under my control but was being driven by the highest level of power.

On the jet returning to the United States, the man sitting next to me started up a conversation. He was a middle-aged businessman with one of those potbellies that seemed ready to burst. We chatted about numerous subjects and finally about native Australians. I told him of my experience in the Outback. He listened intently, but his concluding remarks seemed to sum up the response I had been receiving. He said, "Well, no one knew these people even existed, and if they are leaving, well so what? Frankly, I don't think anyone will give a damn! Besides that," he added, "it's their ideas against ours, and can a whole society of people be wrong?"

For several weeks my thoughts about the wonderful Real People were gift-wrapped and sealed tightly inside my heart and behind my lips. These people had touched my life so deeply that it was almost like "casting pearls before swine" to risk the negative reaction I felt might be forthcoming. Gradually, however, I began to realize my old friends were genuinely interested. Some asked me to speak about my unique experience to groups. The response was always the same; listeners sitting spellbound, people who realize what has been done cannot be undone, but can be changed.

True, the Real People tribe were leaving, but their message is left to us, even with our gravy and cake-frosting lifestyles and attitudes. Not that we want to talk the tribe into staying, into having more children. That is none of our business. What we should care about is putting their peaceful, meaningful values into practical application. I now know we each have two lives: the one we learn by and the one we live after that. The time has come to listen to the frightened moans of our fellow brothers and sisters and indeed the earth itself in pain.

Perhaps the future of the world would be in better hands if we forgot about discovering something new and concentrated on recovering our past.

The tribe does not criticize our modern inventions. They honor the fact that human beingness is an experience of expression, creativity, and adventure. But they do believe that in seeking knowledge Mutants need to include the sentence, "If it is in the highest good for all of life everywhere." They hope we will reevaluate our material possessions and adapt them accordingly. They also believe humankind is closer to experiencing paradise then ever before. We have the technology to feed every person in the world and the knowledge to provide a means of self-expression, self-worth, shelter, and more, for all people everywhere if we wish to do so.

With encouragement and support from my children and close friends, I began to put my Outback experience into writing and also began speaking anywhere I was invited, for civic organizations, prisons, churches, schools, and so on. The response was split. The KKK referred to me as the enemy; another white-supremacy group in Idaho put racial messages on all the cars in the parking lot at my speaking location. Some ultraconservative Christians received my lecture by telling me they believe the Outback nation to be pagans destined for hell. Four employees of a leading Australian television probe program flew to the United States, hid in a closet at a lecture, and attempted to discredit everything I said. They were certain no Aborigines had escaped the census and still lived in the wild. They called me a fraud. But a wonderful balance took place. For every nasty comment, there was someone else eager to learn about mental telepathy, how to replace weapons with illusion, and to hear in depth the values and techniques the Real People use in their lifestyle.

People ask how this experience has changed my life. My answer is, Profoundly. After I returned to the United States my father passed away. I was there holding his hand, loving and supporting him on his journey. The day after the funeral I asked my stepmother for something to remember him by—a cufflink, a tie, an old hat, anything. She refused. "There isn't anything for you," she said. Instead of reacting with bitterness as I once might have done, I responded by mentally blessing the dear soul, and I left my parents' home for the last time, proud of my own beingness; looking up at the clear blue sky, I winked at my dad.

I now believe there would have been no lesson available to me if my stempother had lovingly said, "Certainly. This house is full of your parents' things. Take something to remind you of your father." That is what I expected. My growth came when I was denied what was rightfully mine and I recognized the duality. The Real People told me the only way to pass a test is to take the test. I am now at the point in my life when I can observe an opportunity to pass a spiritual test even though the situation appears very negative. I have learned the difference between observing what is taking place and judging it. I have learned that everything is an opportunity for spiritual enrichment.

Recently, someone who had heard me lecture wanted to introduce me to a man from Hollywood. It was January, in Missouri, a cold snowy night. We had dinner, and I spent hours talking while Roger and the other guests sat eating and drinking coffee. The following morning he called to discuss the possibility of making a movie.

"Where did you go last night?" he asked. "We were paying the bill, getting our coats, and saying good-bye when someone pointed out you had disappeared. We looked outside but you had just vanished; there wasn't even a footprint in the snow!"

"Yes," I replied. My answer formed in my mind like an idea written in newly processed concrete. "I intend to spend the rest of my life using the knowledge I learned in the Outback. Everything! Even the magic of illusion!"

"I, Burnam Burnam, an Aboriginal Australian of the Wurundjeri tribe, do hereby declare that I have read every word of the book *Mutant Message Down Under.*

"It is the first book in my life's experience that I have read nonstop from cover to cover. I did so with great excitement and respect. It is a classic and does not violate any trust given to its author by us Real People. Rather it portrays our value systems and esoteric insights in such a way as to make me feel extremely proud of my heritage.

"In telling the world of your experiences, you have righted an historical wrong. In the seventeenth century the English explorer William Dampier wrote of us as being the 'most primitive, wretched people on the face of this earth.' *Mutant Message* uplifts us into a higher plane of consciousness and makes us the regal and majestic people that we are."

—*Letter from Burnam Burnam,*
a Wurundjeri elder